He'd dressed casually in white linen pants and a light blue button-up that fit his muscled body just enough to make her mouth water.

"Those are beautiful," she said, eyeing the flowers but really thinking about the width of his shoulders and taut flatness of his abdomen.

He held the bouquet out to her. "I may not live here permanently, but I'm still a Southern gentleman. My grandmother would skin me if I didn't bring flowers to my date."

Jasmine chuckled and took the flowers from him, her heart skipping a little at the mention of this being a date. The sweet fragrance wrapped around her the way she wanted Kevin's arms to embrace her. "Is your grandmother the only reason I got flowers?" she teased.

She turned and took the flowers over to the dresser. There wasn't a vase in the room, but there was a vanity pitcher and bowl on the dresser. She grabbed the pitcher and put the flowers inside, setting it next to her bed.

"That, and when I saw them, I thought of you. Bright, colorful, happy."

Dear Reader,

There are a lot of negative stereotypes about men with multiple kids. My goal with *Guarding His Heart* was to show a positive image of a blended family. Kevin may have come across as a playboy in the other books, but I hope you see there is more to Kevin. He's devoted to his family and has a great capacity for love—something he has to realize as his feelings for Jasmine grow.

Jasmine is fun and spunky. Her personality immediately jives with Kevin's, but she has her own concerns to get over before she can accept the love Kevin offers. She's a complicated woman with a unique set of needs that Kevin isn't afraid to step in and help with.

I hope you enjoy *Guarding His Heart*. I'm hard at work on the final Scoring for Love book. Get ready for Will Hampton to settle down.

Sincerely,

Synithia

GUARDING
His Heart

SYNITHIA WILLIAMS

HARLEQUIN® KIMANI™ ROMANCE

Recycling programs
for this product may
not exist in your area.

ISBN-13: 978-1-335-21676-2

Guarding His Heart

Copyright © 2018 by Synithia R. Williams

For questions and comments about the quality of this book please contact us
at CustomerService@Harlequin.com.

H HARLEQUIN®
™ www.Harlequin.com

Printed in U.S.A.

Synithia Williams has been an avid romance-novel lover since picking up her first at the age of thirteen. It was only natural that she would begin penning her own romances soon after—much to the chagrin of her high school math teachers. She's a native of South Carolina and now writes romances as hot as their Southern settings. Outside of writing she works on water quality and sustainability issues for local government. She's married to her own personal hero, and they have two sons who've convinced her that professional wrestling and superheroes are supreme entertainment. When she isn't working, writing or being a wife and mother, she's usually bingeing on TV series, playing around on social media or planning her next girls' night out with friends. You can learn more about Synithia by visiting her website, www.synithiawilliams.com, where she blogs about writing, life and relationships.

Books by Synithia Williams

Harlequin Kimani Romance

A New York Kind of Love
A Malibu Kind of Romance
Full Court Seduction
Overtime for Love
Guarding His Heart

To you for picking up this book
and taking this ride with me.

Acknowledgments

Thank you to Chenille, Sam and Cindy for sharing
your experiences living with juvenile diabetes and
being in a relationship with someone with the
condition. I hope I gave an accurate reflection in this
book with Jasmine and Kevin's relationship. Thanks
to the editorial staff at Harlequin Kimani Romance
for helping me flesh out the characters of this story.
Finally, writing a book is hard. I couldn't have
finished this book without the support of a great set
of writer friends. Whether for virtual hugs, words of
encouragement or listening to me rant, the Divas
are always there. You ladies are much appreciated.

Chapter 1

Kevin Koucky had no problem getting naked.

Getting naked in a cold studio, in front of a crowd of mostly strangers, as part of the photo shoot for *Sports Fitness* magazine was an entirely different situation. He glanced at his publicist across the studio. Rod gave Kevin two thumbs-up while his always enthusiastic grin covered his thin face.

Kevin answered with a half smile. Rod had been raving about this photo shoot ever since the magazine had called with the offer. Kevin's naked body was about to grace the cover of a magazine hitting every magazine rack in the country. The "Bodies in Motion" issue, which paid homage to the various fitness levels of professional athletes, was the magazine's most popular of the year. The cover spot was given to someone considered to be at the top of their game. Kevin had played professional basketball since he was eighteen and was proud of being considered an elite athlete chosen for the cover. Even if nature was slowly siphoning away his abilities.

The representative for *Sports Fitness* walked over to him. The petite brunette had a friendly face underlaid with a fierce focus toward ensuring he was comfortable as they prepared for the shoot.

"Okay, Kevin," she said. "Jasmine is here, and she's ready."

Kevin looked at his wrist to check the time. Realized a second later it wasn't there because he was butt naked in a cold studio. They'd been waiting fifteen minutes for the diva photographer to make her way uptown and complete the shoot. He'd never meet Jasmine Hook before, but she was already getting on his nerves. He wasn't in the mood to deal with an artist who had a self-importance complex and believed coming to a photo shoot late somehow increased her demand.

"Oh, she finally decided to show up," Kevin said, not bothering to hide his annoyance.

The representative's grin tightened. "Well, she had another appointment before this that ran long and then got caught in traffic."

Kevin looked skyward. "Yeah, I'm sure her time photographing models and actors provides her with plenty of perfect excuses for being fashionably late." He'd heard enough about Jasmine to know she was the most sought-after fashion photographer in the nation. Why she was chosen for this shoot probably had more to do with her name than anything. He wouldn't be surprised to find she was just as self-absorbed and obsessed with fashion as the people she photographed.

"You'd be surprised how much I've learned photo-was thirty-six years old. Ancient in professional sports. The time had come for plan B.

Whatever the hell that was.

"I want you to show my athleticism," he said. "I'm old compared to the other guys on my team. Show that my age doesn't mean I've lost something." That his body wasn't breaking down.

Her brown eyes narrowed slightly. She nodded slowly. He got the sneaking suspicion she could see into him and had read his thoughts. His fears. Or, maybe, he just liked the way she looked at him.

"I think I can do that." She reached with her left hand and scratched the back of her shoulder.

The white shirt lifted with the movement. He caught a flash of a ring in her belly button against smooth caramel skin. He sucked in a breath, his ab muscles tightening. Jasmine didn't seem to notice how he stilled at the flash of her belly ring. She'd turned away and rummaged through her bag.

Just like that, he was hooked. The need to discover what else was pierced tempted him like a hunt for the treasures of the universe. He wanted to take his time uncovering all of her secrets. Did tattoos accompany her piercings? His arms, chest and back were plastered with body art, each one significant to him in some way. He had no problems with women doing the same, but he liked that Jasmine hadn't covered all of her sexy brown skin. That would make discovering what, if any, spots she'd decorated even more fun.

She turned with another camera gadget in her hand and faced him. "So, Kevin, are you ready to get naked for me?"

Considering he was there specifically to be photographed naked and she was a photographer, the words shouldn't have sent heat shooting through his veins with the force of a charging bull. Coming from her full lips, in her silky voice, with that spark of hidden wildness in her eye, not only was heat charging full steam, but another area rose to half-mast.

Smiling, Kevin unhooked his towel and let it drop to the floor. "Any damn time."

Jasmine didn't blush or frown. She boldly looked over his body. Her gaze paused below his waistline. The flash of appreciation that lit her eye made him want to crow like a rooster. Forced thoughts of the drills coach ran them through in practice was the only thing keeping him from getting a full-on erection. His pride wouldn't let him show her just how much her look made his pulse race.

Her dark eyes met his and she cocked a brow. "Let's do this."

Jasmine had photographed tons of half- and completely naked people in her career. Some of the most beautiful women, the hottest men and captivating celebrities. It was almost impossible to have a career as a fashion photographer and not encounter beautiful, naked people. But never before had she had such a hard time focusing on capturing the scene instead of how utterly incredible the subject looked naked.

She'd appreciated a nice body before. Even accepted an offer or two from people she'd photographed with a no-strings, no-commitment caveat.

As long as there was little chance of messy drama during or afterward. She wasn't currently looking for anything long-term or even casual. She had other goals at the moment. But her brain was barely letting her separate the job of photographing Kevin from her primal appreciation of his body.

Her woman parts were attracted to everything about him. The man was a work of art. Long lean muscles and tan skin decorated with beautifully drawn tattoos. At first glance, his intense gaze and large muscular body were intimidating. But then his lips cracked a come-here-and-get-all-of-this smile accompanied by a twinkle in his eye that promised hours of I-shouldn't-have-done-that-but-damn-he-was-good memories.

Only by the grace of God did she survive the photo shoot without drooling down her chest. She had a lot going on right now. She'd finally gotten Angelo to agree to let her exhibit at his gallery at the end of the year. Which meant she actually had an end result after telling the fashion world she was no longer going to photograph beautiful people for a lot of money and instead follow more artistic pursuits.

Despite the skepticism her announcement had received, she was excited. She'd made her money and built her career. She'd earned the right to do what she wanted. Kevin, though very pretty and tempting, was not part of the way she needed to spend her last few nights in New York.

"Was it as good for you as it was for me?"

Kevin's voice caressed her body like a warm ocean breeze. She could almost forgive him for such a cheesy line. Almost.

She stopped packing her camera to look up at him. She was tall at five foot nine. In her black boots, she brushed six feet, but she still had to tilt her head back to meet his eyes. And there went her pulse, accelerating from the eye contact. He'd wrapped the towel back around his waist, but his incredible chest and forearms were bare. Despite the cold room, heat radiated off him in waves. That, or her body temperature rose in his presence.

"Do you really think you're the first person who's tried that line with me?" She leaned back against the table and rested her hands on the top.

"I don't care who's tried it in the past. I want to know if it's working for me today."

His confidence was a turn-on. She was drawn to sexy, confident men. Discovering whether the confidence was warranted or just overcompensation was fun to figure out. She had a feeling Kevin's was warranted.

"Working for you in what way?" she asked.

"Is it increasing the likelihood I'll be able to see you again?"

She tilted her head to the side. "How is photographing you today supposed to make me want to see you again?"

He shifted his weight and rubbed his hands together. The movement made the towel dip lower. Her gaze dipped before she could stop herself. When she met his eyes again, he lifted a brow.

Yeah, you look good and yeah, I know it.

"You were behind the camera," Kevin said. "That's very impersonal. I thought you'd want a more up close experience."

Seriously? Was that all it took for this man to get a woman in his bed? She didn't doubt it. Hell, her body was responding, her nipples hardening and heat building in the apex of her thighs just from the promise in his eyes. The man was the embodiment of dangerous sex appeal with those dark eyes, tattoos, muscles and good looks. A combination that had caused women to make regrettable decisions since the beginning of time.

"Oh, no need. My camera has a zoom lens, you see. I've already got an up close and personal view of everything I wanted to see."

His smile scattered her thoughts for a second. "And you're not interested in seeing more?"

She was definitely interested in seeing more. If she didn't have plans for tonight, and she didn't have to start packing to leave New York, and she had a little more time to feel him out and decide if he was worthy of getting in her bed, she would have said yes.

Not going to bed with Kevin was good for other reasons. Guys like Kevin had the pesky potential to become more than just a fling if she wasn't careful. Guys like him got in her blood, her head and before long, had her thinking she was in love right when he was ready to move on.

"I'm sure it would be fun, Kevin, but I'm going have to say no, thank you." She didn't smile with her letdown but kept her voice casual. Kevin seemed flirty and laidback, but she'd witnessed how volatile some guys could be when faced with rejection or how others would view an accompanying smile as an excuse to keep hounding.

He raised a brow. "You sure?"

She took a deep breath and gave him one last once-over. Yeah, Kevin would definitely be fun, but she didn't have time for that kind of detour. "I'm sure."

He placed a hand over his heart and stepped back. "You break my heart, Jasmine, but I won't push."

Score more points for him not behaving like an idiot. "I appreciate that."

"I'm in town for a few days. You change your mind, give me a call."

If only she were in town a few days. "I don't have your number."

The man miraculously pulled a pen from his towel. The towel shifted dangerously low, so low she could see the dusting of hair below his waist. Magically it held in place.

"You have an ink pen in your towel?"

He chuckled and stepped close. "Always be ready." He took her hand in his. His was large and warm but surprisingly gentle.

Heat zipped up her arm and through her chest, right down to her toes. There was a hint of cologne combined with an underlying peppery spice that heated her even more. He turned her hand palm up, uncapped the pen with his mouth and wrote a number on her wrist.

The movement of the pen tickled. The heat of his fingers branded her. Her pulse fluttered and her breathing stuttered in her chest.

His eyes lifted to hers. Desire and a dare flickering in their depths. He lifted her arm higher, blew on the ink. Goose bumps rose all over her body. Her sex tingled and her nipples tightened.

"You've got it now," he said in a low voice she felt all the way in her toes. Kevin ran his thumb over the number, smiled at her, then dropped her hand. "Call me."

He turned and walked away. The towel dipped. Jasmine sucked in a breath. He caught it before it fell. Jasmine released a disappointed breath. Yeah, he was definitely a get-in-your-blood kind of guy. Thank goodness she was leaving New York in two weeks.

Now, to keep from calling him before she left town.

Chapter 2

"Come on, Kevin, tell me. Are you retiring?"

Kevin chuckled and took a sip of the red wine in his hand. He leaned against the balcony of photographer Rafael Sim's penthouse overlooking uptown Manhattan. He stretched out his hands reflexively. The nearly constant ache didn't subside. Pretty soon he wouldn't be able to ignore it. He put down the glass of wine and looked up from his failing hands.

"Rafael, when the decision is made, I'll let you know."

"You really think you have one more season left in you?" Rafael asked. There was no judgment in his voice. If anything, there was a hint of admiration in his friend's tone.

A month ago, Kevin would have lived up to that admiration.

"I'm not quite ready to be put out to pasture," Kevin said. Carefully, he picked up the wineglass and took another sip. He didn't admit defeat easily and he wasn't ready to give up his place in the league.

"Well, you know retiring will free up your time to pursue other things," Rafael said. His curly dark hair was cut in a fashionable style that would have looked ridiculous on any other guy, but Rafael was able to pull it off, along with his white pants, flowered button-up shirt and dark-rimmed glasses. That was Rafael, fashionable to the core.

"Things like what?"

Rafael shrugged and leaned his forearms on the balcony next to Kevin. "Things like sponsoring the art exhibit of your good friend."

Kevin laughed at the blatant request. He'd met Rafael several years ago during New York Fashion Week. That was right after Kevin's divorce, when he'd chosen to bury his heartbreak in the arms of a supermodel he'd met. She'd dragged him to a fashion show and instead of being bored out of his mind, he'd ended up sitting next to Rafael, talking about art. Kevin had agreed to sponsor Rafael's next exhibit and they'd been friends ever since.

"You know I got you," Kevin said. "What are you showcasing this time?"

"Chronicling life in my hometown in Texas. The place once thrived… Now the jobs are gone and it's dying out. My family is still there, and they're trying to hold on like everyone else." Rafael's voice was bittersweet. "The loss of jobs is sad, but the hope of the people still shines, ya know?"

"I know." Kevin's own hometown in South Carolina had gone through the same thing. Loss of industry, people moving out and a stunted tax base had nearly killed the place his mom and grandmother still called home. He'd done what he could to help bring business back and the place was finally making a comeback. "I think that's a good idea. Maybe it'll help shine some light on your hometown."

Rafael nodded. "That's what I'm hoping for."

The sound of conversation inside the penthouse increased. Kevin straightened and glanced toward the door. "Sounds like we're missing your party," he teased. There were other people on the balcony, too. Music played from the speakers and conversation and laughter flowed, but it definitely sounded like something had excited the people inside.

"I know," Rafael straightened and walked toward the balcony doors. "Let's go see what's going on."

Kevin followed. He glanced through the glass at the people still inside. He spotted a pair of beautiful brown eyes and a flash of blue-tipped hair. A slow smile spread over his face while pleasant surprise and the thrill of a chase played a pickup game in his chest. "Jasmine Hook."

Rafael nodded and grinned. "She made it."

Kevin glanced at Rafael. "You know her?" Obviously, if she was here. He wanted to know how Rafael knew the woman he'd thought of repeatedly since the shoot earlier that day.

"We worked a couple of shoots together. How do you know her?" Rafael threw Kevin a curious look.

"She photographed me this morning."

Rafael's eyes widened. He ran his hand through the curly bangs that had fallen over his eyes. "No shit. She saw you naked." He didn't say anything else, but his tone begged Kevin to spill some dirt.

"She did, but she wasn't impressed."

Rafael flicked his wrist. "I should have known. Jasmine isn't easily impressed. She dated Julio for a while and they broke up about two years ago. After that, she hasn't gone out much. I was hoping you and your raw animal magnetism would have broken her dry spell."

Kevin seemed to recall that Julio was Rafael's cousin. He wasn't in fashion but he was a popular DJ in the New York club circuit. "What happened with her and Julio?"

He had expected his *animal magnetism* to have gotten Jasmine to at least agree to see him again. He didn't typically strike out when it came to women. He wasn't arrogant, but he also knew some women were easily drawn to a professional athlete. A lesson he'd learned the hard and fast way early in his career.

"He got back with his kid's mom. They're married now."

"He broke her heart?" That would explain why she'd backed off. Broken hearts made getting back out there difficult. He knew; he'd been on both ends of that particular ailment.

"Doubtful," Rafael said. "She seemed okay afterward. None of the usual dramatics, and she's still okay with me." Rafael shrugged as if that explained everything.

"Why wouldn't she be okay with you?" He didn't bother to ask what the usual dramatics were. Rafael was a bit of a drama king himself. Last year, Kevin witnessed one of Rafael's post-breakup meltdowns. That had not been pretty.

"I hooked them up," Rafael explained. He pulled open the door and stepped inside. "Come with me to greet her," he said over his shoulder.

Kevin followed Rafael over to Jasmine. She looked even better hours later. She seemed chill and relaxed as she greeted Rafael's other guests. Her smile was easy and her laughter infectious. She still wore the black boots from earlier with a different pair of jeans, torn this time, and a gray tank with MTWTFSS on the front. Days of the week, the WTF in the middle in bold. Kevin smiled at the hidden question.

Rafael strolled right up to Jasmine and encased her in a huge bear hug. Jasmine laughed and hugged him right back. The two were obviously friends. Whatever ill will she had toward Rafael's cousin had not spilled over and ruined their relationship.

She glanced at Kevin over Rafael's shoulder. Surprise flashed across her features. He didn't know what divine intervention put her at the same house party as him, but he was thankful for it. He acknowledged her with a nod of his head. She blessed him with one of her killer smiles before she pulled back and looked at Rafael.

"I hear you got a good look at Kevin's goodies," Rafael teased.

Jasmine's answering chuckle made various parts of Kevin's body tighten. "He did well. Not a trace of shame or embarrassment in the middle of a room full of strangers." Her brown eyes met his. The light hit them, adding a golden hint to their brown depths. He wanted to step closer to gauge their hidden secrets. "I didn't expect to see you here," she said to Kevin.

Rafael answered before Kevin. "He's a good friend of mine. Even more so today because he agreed to sponsor my next exhibit." A woman across the room called Rafael's name. He turned toward her and nodded. "Well, since you two know each other, I'll go see what Livie wants." He waved his hands at her and Kevin as if they should keep talking and left them.

Jasmine turned the full impact of her sexy smile Kevin's way. The dull ache in his hands was easily forgotten when she smiled at him that way. Everything was forgotten except thoughts of what he might need to do to see that smile more often.

"So, exhibit sponsor, huh?" she said with a raised brow. "Maybe I should call you."

"I like Rafael's work. I haven't seen yours." He actually had and knew it was good. The pictures they'd gone over after the shoot were impressive. He knew the "Bodies in Motion" issue wasn't just about gratuitous naked athletes, but she'd done a great job of capturing his athleticism as he'd run, jumped and dunked the basketball in the studio. She was talented, but he liked teasing her.

"You're an art critic now?" She brushed her long, blue-tipped bangs out of her eyes and met his gaze through thick lashes. The silver bangles on her slim wrist slid down her arm almost to her elbow.

He pursed his lips and nodded to try to look serious. "Oh yes. I'm very selective. My opinion is highly sought after by those in the know."

Full lips twitched and her eyes brightened with laughter. "Hmm. I'll have to keep that in mind. I can't have you criticizing my photos of you."

"Yours will be judged extra hard."

He placed his hand near her lower back but didn't touch and nodded his head in the direction of the bar on the left side of Rafael's spacious living room. There wasn't a bartender and Rafael's guests could mix their own drinks. Jasmine let him lead the way. He was pretty sure *let* was the right word. He doubted she would ever let anyone direct her if she didn't want them to.

"And why will mine be judged harder than the others?"

"Because they're pictures of me," he said. "I never like my pictures."

She laughed as if that were ludicrous and he grinned, drawn in by the music of her voice. It was true, though. He didn't like pictures of himself. He knew women found him attractive, but he wasn't classically handsome. He'd filled in his tall lanky frame with muscles and covered his upper body in art, but that didn't make up for his prominent brow and not-perfectly symmetrical features. He hadn't been popular with the ladies until he'd excelled at basketball and ultimately gone professional.

"What I saw though my camera says you have nothing to be ashamed of." She reached for the bottle of red wine and poured herself a drink.

"Oh, so you did like what you saw?"

She glanced at him from the corner of her eye, the hint of a smile on her lips. "That's just my professional opinion, you understand. Purely an academic observation."

His answering chuckle eased him deeper into her spell. She was cool. Funny and lively in a way that immediately made him want to relax and get to know her better. "Okay, academic." He took her free hand in his, pretended he didn't feel the spark that came from her skin against his and turned her hand over. "Then why can I still see my number on your wrist?"

She sucked in a breath as if the spark had hit her, too, but shrugged easily. "I have no idea. You must have used some super permanent ink when you wrote it down."

He'd used a regular pen. She hadn't washed it away. Which meant she'd at least considered calling him. Which meant he had a chance. "You know, I think I did." He rubbed his thumb over the soft skin where his number still resided.

Her body shivered and her eyes darkened. With hunger? Awareness? Maybe desire? He wasn't sure which but hoped for all three. She slipped her arm back. "I'll scrub it off later."

"After you write my number down so you can call me." He eased closer.

She smelled delicious. Sweet and decadent like fruit and chocolate. Was that perfume or just her? One way to find out was to hold her naked. Learn all her curves and cravings. Follow the trail across her neck and breasts to discover each and every hidden secret she had.

His heart beat an intoxicating rhythm in his chest. The anticipation coursing through him slowly rose as if he were about to go on an expedition, and Jasmine was the ultimate experience.

"Who says I'm going to call you?" There was no heat in her voice, just a trace of flirtation.

Kevin's grin widened. Oh hell yes. He definitely had a shot. "Who says you aren't?"

She sipped her wine, licking her lips after pulling the glass away, and hit him with a look that was both flirty and don't-get-ahead-of-yourself. She was interested but maybe still weighing her options. Cool, he didn't have a problem with a woman who took her time to make a decision. If she had standards he needed to meet, then he would do whatever he needed in order to meet them.

Rafael clapped and got everyone's attention before

Jasmine could reply. Reluctantly, Kevin gave him his attention, too.

"Okay, folks, you know what time it is?" Rafael asked.

A collective, half-hearted groan combined with muffled laughter in the room. Kevin looked at Jasmine, who rolled her eyes and chuckled. She said at the same time as him and everyone else in the room: "Game time."

Rafael loved playing games when he got people together. "You got that right," he said cheerfully. "We'll start with Cards Against Humanity."

Jasmine raised her wineglass in a salute. "I love that game."

Kevin tapped his chest. "Me, too."

"We're such horrible people." She bit her lower lip and they both laughed.

Damn, he really liked her. The game's tagline did say it was the card game for terrible people. Mostly because some of the questions and answers in the cards were so outrageous he wouldn't dare play it around his mother or grandmother.

They joined the rest of Rafael's guests who agreed to play. Jasmine had a sense of humor that matched his own.

After the card game, Rafael decided they'd all play Two Truths and a Lie. Each person told three stories and the rest of the room had to guess which story was the lie. Learning that Jasmine had skinny-dipped in her gym back in high school only added to the wild mystery of her.

After the games concluded, the crowd was even more relaxed and talkative. He and Jasmine stuck together as they mingled with Rafael's mixture of artistic friends. They eventually broke away into their own conversations about art, music and movies before ending up in a corner on the balcony.

"I still can't believe you've never seen *The Princess Bride*," Jasmine said, shaking her head as if he were an enigma.

"Why would I ever see that movie?" he asked, unable to control his humor at her audacity.

"Because it's a freaking classic, that's why." She slapped his chest. The low light of the balcony played on the muscles in her arms as she moved. He had discovered a tattoo. A small heart on the front of her shoulder that occasionally peaked out from the strap of her tank top in her enthusiasm.

He slid closer to her and ran his hand over the smooth stone of the balcony railing until his fingertips brushed hers. "*The Blues Brothers* is a classic. A princess movie is not."

"You're such a guy," she said with mock disgust. She brushed her bangs away. "You could learn a lot about romance by watching a princess movie." She took a sip from a bottle of water. His gaze dropped to her neck. So sleek and sexy. Even her shoulders were hot. Everything about her had his body on edge.

He slipped his hand over hers. The air thickened with the heat vibrating between them. "I know plenty about romance."

She sucked in a breath and licked her lips. "What did *The Blues Brothers* teach you about romance?"

He tilted his head to the side and leaned in close to her. "Right now, the only thing I can think of is having a mission from God."

She rolled her eyes but continued smiling. "What mission is that?"

He didn't know if she recognized the quote from the movie or not, but right now, he felt like heaven was telling him to kiss this woman. "To do this."

He covered her mouth with his.

Chapter 3

His kiss was soft and gentle. But the power of his body was a constant vibration of energy beneath his skin. The promise of a passionate explosion simmered in the easy touch.

It was a player's kiss. Sexy and teasing enough to make her want to lean in for more. The kind of kiss that brought fantasies of his lips caressing other parts of her body. He didn't grope her or jerk her up against his body. Only his lips touched hers, and that made her yearn more than she had when she'd tried giving up coffee and potato chips cold turkey two years ago.

Then, as if he knew she was a second away from latching onto him the way she had the coffee and the bag of kettle-cooked salt and vinegar chips her sister brought to convince her to give up the madness, he eased back. Her eyelids were like weights as she slowly lifted them to meet his eyes.

The corner of his mouth was lifted cockily. His eyes

held the intense focus of a hunter closing in on prey. Excitement and possession swirled in their depths. If she let herself, she'd agree to the affair he offered with just a look.

Except she had goals. Professional and personal ones. Her own exhibit. No relationship drama. No more getting caught up in the lies of a promised forever.

"What are you thinking about?" His voice was silky and mellow. Her thighs clenched with need.

Your exhibit. Remember your exhibit.

"Cabins," she said.

He blinked several times. "Cabins?" He ran a hand over his lower lip. "Why are you thinking about cabins?"

Probably not the best lead-in after a fantastic kiss, but he needed to be brought down a notch or two. Kevin had thrown out the bait with that sexy-as-hell-but-not-quite-enough kiss, and she'd bitten. She could tell he was ready to lure her in, and oh, she wanted to be lured. Really, really wanted to be, but her life was about goals, not getting off.

"My next project. I want to document cabins."

Kevin's brow cocked. He still smiled but there was a definite dimming of the spark in his eye.

"I'm trying to focus on my next project," she said. "You would distract me from that."

"Ahh, now I get it." He took half a step back. Just out of her reach. She ran her hands over her pant legs to stop herself from reaching out.

He leaned an elbow on the balcony. Nailed her with his full attention. "Tell me about your project."

He couldn't be serious? Could he? She hadn't said that to make him run, but she hadn't expected him to ask for more information. "Why?"

"Obviously, your project is important enough to distract you from what I thought was a damn good kiss." He raised a brow in question.

She nodded, willing to concede to the truth. "The kiss was very good."

"Yet you thought of cabins. I want to know about the project."

"Seriously?" She'd expected some sly comment about him not being a distraction, or that they could just have a little fun before she moved on. Instead he'd asked for more information. Kevin was making it hard for her to not leave New York with a bang.

He waved a hand for her to continue. "Seriously. I'd like to get to know you."

Jasmine eyed him and tried to tell if he was full of crap. He watched her expectantly. Eyes focused. The seductive up-tilt of his mouth was still there. Still tempting.

Fine. If he wanted to know, she'd tell him. If he thought her idea was dumb, then she'd save a lot of time trying to figure out if he was worth her serious consideration and move on quickly. If he liked the idea… maybe leaving New York with a bang, literally, wasn't such a bad idea.

She took a deep breath. When she'd announced her plans to a few people in the fashion industry, they'd looked at her as if she'd announced she was packing up and moving to Alaska to become a pioneer woman. Maybe she was taking a drastic step, but she wanted to do something worthwhile. She didn't care what they thought, but the idea of Kevin looking at her like that? Well, that made her stomach churn a little.

"Okay, so I was visiting relatives in Georgia last year," she said in a rush before changing her mind.

"When I was there, my uncle had a bonfire out in the field next to the house. They used to grow corn there I think, but anyway, there was this old cabin along the edge of the field. When I asked, he said it was the first house his great-great-grandfather built during the Reconstruction. He'd purchased the small bit of land, farmed it, fought the Klan on it and ultimately survived."

"Damn. That's cool as hell." Excitement and interest infused Kevin's voice.

"I know, right?" Her own excitement was piqued by his. She'd been thrilled to learn more about her mother's family. She'd lost her mom when she was so young. Her dad remarried and she'd rarely spent time with her mother's family. After her father later divorced and her stepmother completely disappeared out of her life, Jasmine had reached out to her mother's family.

"So I took pictures of the place. Started a scrapbook with the family history I got from my uncle. I sent a copy to him. Then the rest of my family asked for copies. It gave me an idea to capture more old cabins and homes owned by black people. Capture where they lived and highlight their history with what I can track down. Kinda chronicling the everyday life of the regular people trying to make their way in a world that didn't want them to find a way."

"That's what's up." Kevin nodded and sounded impressed. "Where are you starting?"

His response fueled her excitement even more. She'd gotten such a lackluster response from some of her colleagues. Kevin got what she was trying to do. That meant others had to get it, too.

"I'm going back to Georgia. I've been in contact

with a historian who's working to save slave cabins. I'm setting up a meeting with him to get an idea of where to go next."

"What will you do after you finish?" All of the flirtation was gone, replaced by a genuine interest in her project.

"I have an agreement with Jordan and Jones to publish my findings." That was the first time she'd said that out loud. Her disbelief at the leeway the publishing house was giving her seeped into her voice. "Angelero Gallery gave me the okay to exhibit my pictures once I'm done to build up interest before the book's release date."

"Wow. You've got everything lined up."

She did, yet nerves still turned her stomach into a jumbled mess. She had the book deal because of her borrowed status photographing celebrities. The agreement from the gallery was for the same reasons—that and she was friends with the owner. That didn't mean people would like the photos or get what she was trying to convey.

She kept having a recurring nightmare of people only seeing old, dilapidated houses instead of the stories of the people who lived there. What those families overcame. She'd be laughed out of the gallery and her book would flop harder than a deflated basketball.

"I'm excited about the project," she said brightly, instead of letting him hear her insecurities.

"It's cool you have a plan and know what you want. Seriously, not everyone has that."

Something in his voice made her think he didn't refer to people in general, but instead to himself. "What are you doing during the off-season? Do you relax or are you itching for the new season to start?"

He looked down at his hands and stretched them out. A frown pulled on his lips. "Actually, I'm trying to figure out my next steps."

Next steps? From the little she knew of basketball, he was still considered an elite player in the league. "What do you mean?"

"Retirement or not." He looked up at her.

"Retirement? You can't be serious. You just won a championship. You're the cover model for the *Sports Fitness* 'Bodies in Motion' issue. That only goes to top athletes. Why would you retire?" Okay, so maybe she'd researched him a little after today's shoot.

"I'm thirty-six. Might as well go out while I'm still on top." He shrugged as if the answer was an obvious one.

Except the look in his eye didn't match his voice. His tone reminded her of someone forcing themselves to make a decision they were still unsure about. "What will you do if you retire?"

He shrugged. "That's the thing. I've got a few business interests. I could explore more of those options. It's just…"

"They're not basketball."

He studied his hands again. "Basketball has been my life since I was eighteen. I was drafted right in the middle of my first year of college and I haven't thought about doing anything else since. Could I really be happy in a suit, sitting behind a desk at a corporation?"

She couldn't see him in corporate America. Not because of the tattoos or pierced ears; the art could be hidden beneath business suits and the earrings could come out. She couldn't see it because Kevin had this layer of wildness and excitement about him. No matter the environment, that dangerous air and flair to live outside the boundaries expected of him would always show.

But stranger things had happened. She didn't really know him and was basing her decision on his outgoing personality and the few reports of his off-court antics she'd read. The guy took his teammates skydiving to celebrate their first playoff win.

But he was thirty-six and successful. Her quick internet search hadn't brought up rumors of him spending money frivolously or filing for bankruptcy, a situation that plagued some celebrities who achieved superstardom as young as he had. He could get excited about one of his businesses and really thrive.

"You won't know until you try," she encouraged. "If you're ready to retire, don't let the idea that you're only good at basketball stop you. I'm sure you're good at other things."

"How do you know?" he asked with a sexy tilt of his full lips that made her ease closer.

"Your eyes are intelligent." She met that dark gaze. His eyes were brown, bold and very cocky, but he wasn't a dumb jock. He watched, listened and observed. All signs of intelligence.

His gaze became guarded. His brows drew together. She must have surprised him. "No one's ever told me that."

"I'm glad to be the first."

Kevin closed the distance between them. His large hand clasped her waist. The possessiveness came back to his gaze. Jasmine's pulse accelerated and she swallowed hard. He pulled her close until the tips of her breasts brushed his hard chest. A shiver went down her spine. Not from fear but anticipation. Heat roared through her like wildfire.

"I want to kiss you again."

She wanted to kiss him again. When she didn't protest, his head lowered. Jasmine's lashes lowered, too. Expectation wound up and tightened her nerves like a coiled spring. Thoughts of cabins and next steps in life blew away with the soft breeze.

Ringing filled the air. Something at Kevin's hip vibrated.

He pulled back. "My bad. That's my cell." He pulled out his phone and checked the screen. "My daughter. Let me take this."

Jasmine nodded and stepped back. She tried to steady her breathing as he leaned against the concrete balcony railing and answered the call.

"Hey, babe, what's up?" Kevin frowned and cocked his head. "What? Well, I'm sure your mom has a good reason for saying that." Pause. "Let me talk to her."

Kevin held up a finger toward Jasmine and gave an apologetic shrug. "Sabrina, what's going on?" He listened for a few seconds. His lips tipped up, followed by a low chuckle. A flirty sound filled with history and memories.

She watched Kevin talk to his daughter's mother and her passion slowly cooled. Her internet search had brought up personal information on him, as well. Married young to his high school sweetheart, right when he entered the league. Divorced four years later. After that, he'd been in a long-term relationship with another woman and she'd had twins right before they'd split.

Since then, he hadn't been connected with anyone on a lengthy basis.

Baggage, drama, warning! Back away from this man ASAP.

"Okay, kitten, calm down," he said laughing. "I agree on punishment. She shouldn't have come in late. I'll swing through Atlanta and check out this guy she likes."

He paused to listen. Jasmine's mind whirled. *Kitten?* That was definitely a pet name and had definitely been spoken with affection.

The call ended. He shook his head and slipped the phone in his pocket. "Sorry, that was my ex-wife. My daughter has a new boyfriend and it's driving Sabrina crazy." He turned back and reached for her. "But that's not important right now."

So *kitten* was the ex-wife. Oh no! She wasn't about to sign up for this again.

Jasmine stepped far out of his reach. She looked at her watch. "You know, I've really got a lot to do tomorrow and I need to go."

"Now?"

"Yeah, like, right now." She was having a serious case of déjà vu and that crap wasn't cool. Memories of getting swept up in a guy she knew could get under her skin, ignoring his overly friendly relationship with his ex-wife, the crushing blow when he left her to go back to the familiar. Sure, she didn't have plans to do anything long-term with Kevin, but that didn't mean she wanted to be halftime in whatever game he played with *kitten.*

"But I thought—"

"Kevin, it was really nice to meet you. Good luck in the off-season, okay?" She turned and hurried off the balcony before his smooth lines, sexy smile and sweet kisses made her forget that men always went back to their first loves. She wasn't going to be the rebound chick ever again.

Chapter 4

Two weeks later and Kevin still couldn't get Jasmine out of his mind. He'd swung through Atlanta and checked in on his ex-wife, Sabrina, and their girls. Sabrina always worried their daughters would fall too hard and too fast for a boy and end up brokenhearted.

Kevin couldn't blame her for her fears. He'd broken her heart when they were young. That's why he worked hard to keep his relationships superficial. No more broken hearts in his future if he could help it.

"Why are you frowning?" his grandmother asked.

Kevin looked up at her from his spot on the back porch step. He hadn't heard her exit the house to join him. Every off-season, he spent at least a week or two back home with his mother and grandmother in Silver Springs, South Carolina. Not just because his grandmother made the best red velvet cake in the state.

Charlotte moved a little slower than she used to due to arthritis. Kevin could sympathize with her on that.

Her mind was still sharp, and at eighty-three, she was the person most likely to give him good advice when he needed it.

"Was I frowning?" He stood and took his grandmother's arm.

She tried to shoo him away, but he wasn't to be deterred. She liked to ignore her walker and cane when she was at home. Kevin helped her to one of the rocking chairs on the porch and helped her sit.

"I can walk by myself."

"Yeah, and I can still palm a basketball easily," he replied.

He eased back down onto the top step of the porch. The humidity was at a decent level for a change, making the high temperatures bearable. His grandmother and mother lived together in a house he'd purchased for them in one of the newer subdivisions on a golf course that popped up as part of the town's resurgence. His family lived on a private corner lot that backed up to a natural undisturbed area.

Charlotte huffed and rocked back in the chair. "Is that why you're frowning? You still thinking about that play?"

The play that had almost cost the Gators the championship. The play when the pain and stiffness residing in his hands had gotten so bad he'd dropped the ball and the opposing team scored, tying the game and potentially costing them the win. The play that would have ruined the season if his teammate, Will Hampton, hadn't scored a winning three-point shot right before the buzzer.

"I'm over that, Grandma C," he replied. His grandmother grunted again but didn't dispute him. "I was thinking about Asia. Sabrina's worried about her boyfriend."

"You checked in on them though, right?"

"Yep. He seems like a good kid. I put a little fear in him if he hurts my baby, and I'll drop in more."

"Sabrina's always worried about something," Charlotte mumbled. "Maybe if she stopped worrying, she'd be able to pull that stick out of her ass."

Kevin gave his grandmother a mildly disapproving look. He wouldn't dare to give her an outright glare. Not if he hoped to keep his eyes inside his head. "Grandma, come on. You know she wasn't always like that."

"Well, it's been twelve years since you two divorced. Y'all were too young when you got married anyway. Barely out of high school and right when you were offered a multimillion-dollar contract. I could have told you that was a mistake."

"If I remember correctly, you did."

Charlotte snapped her fingers and pointed at him. "Damn, right. She was the only girl you'd dated. Then you became a star. Don't blame yourself for wanting to see what else was out there. At least you didn't dog her out the way some men might have."

"I know, Grandma C." That still didn't make him feel better.

He'd filed for divorce after four years of marriage. He'd never cheated on Sabrina, but the temptation had been there. His grandmother was right. He'd been young with a lot of money and little experience with women wanting him. So he'd left the marriage instead of cheating, but Sabrina never believed he'd resisted temptation. The years of enjoying the company of beautiful women after their divorce hadn't helped.

They'd managed to salvage their friendship due to both of them wanting to make things easier on their daughters. He would always be there for their two girls.

Five years ago, when Hanna, his girlfriend at the time, gave birth to twins, Sabrina hadn't batted an eye at considering the twins part of her family, even though Hanna's pregnancy had been unexpected, and Sabrina and Hanna hadn't gotten along. He'd been on the verge of ending things with Hanna when she'd gotten pregnant. He may be terrible when it came to relationships, but he'd be damned if he'd be a terrible father.

"Besides," Charlotte continued, "you know what to look for when it comes to no good men. If you say Asia's new boyfriend is decent, then Sabrina should go along with it."

"She did." After he reassured her a dozen times that Asia's boyfriend had no evil plot to break their oldest daughter's heart. "I don't think Asia has to worry about that. She does have to worry about her mom killing her. She's still in trouble for sneaking out to meet him at a party. That's uncalled-for."

He'd made sure Asia understood he wouldn't stand for that either. The car they'd been considering for her sixteenth birthday was firmly off the table. He was especially proud of the way he hadn't wavered when the tears had flown.

Charlotte laughed and patted her legs. "The oldest is always the wild one. At least Paris isn't like that."

Kevin nodded. "Thank heaven for that." Asia's little sister was more into fantasy novels and reading than boys. That might change in a few years, but for now he was thrilled.

"Well, if you calmed down Sabrina, then why were you frowning?"

He shook his head. "No reason."

Grandma C gave great advice, but he didn't discuss his affairs with her. He would figure out a way to see Jasmine again.

He'd held her briefly. That swift touch and quick kiss had gone through his mind almost as frequently as he'd thought about dropping the ball. Both had been recent major disappointments. He was handling the situation with his deteriorating joints, and he would also figure out why Jasmine had run off when there was obviously a spark between them.

"It's a woman, isn't it?" Charlotte asked in a knowing voice. Her piercing gaze held laughter.

He should have known she'd guess the problem anyway. "I know a lot of women," he hedged.

"I see the reports. I know you do. But this woman must be special."

Kevin didn't want to think about the reports his grandmother had seen. He was considered a wild child in the league. The media liked to document his dating life as evidence of his carefree lifestyle. They assumed he dated different women because he liked the playboy lifestyle, not because he refused to get serious and disappoint another woman.

"Can we talk about something else besides women?"

Charlotte leaned back in her seat. The humor didn't leave her expression. "Fine, just don't run off and marry her before I get to meet her."

The idea was so ludicrous Kevin laughed hard enough to bring a tear to his eye. "I am never getting married again."

"That's what you think. He—" she pointed to the sky "—may think differently."

Kevin nodded and looked over the spacious, manicured backyard instead of arguing. He doubted the Big Guy upstairs had a personal interest in his abysmal love life. If that were the case, his marriage would have worked out, or at least his relationship with Hanna.

His mother had prayed hard enough for both. She'd be giving him a lecture about finding love and happiness right now if she hadn't gone to the West Coast to visit the twins.

Kevin preferred to focus on quick flings. No feelings to attach. No expectations of more. He was old enough to admit the marriage to Sabrina hadn't been wise. They'd been young and in love but hadn't really gotten out of their small town to see the world. Things with Hanna had been good, but he hadn't loved her. He didn't think long-term relationships were in the cards for him and he'd accepted that. He didn't have to play baseball to recognize that he'd had two strikes in the relationship department. He wasn't playing to lose.

"I spoke with Robert Taylor yesterday at the grocery store." His grandmother changed the subject. "He says work is almost complete on the new community center. That's going to be great when it opens. Exactly what the town needs. He told me to thank you for the donation."

"Mayor Taylor doesn't have to thank me. This is my hometown. I'm happy to help." Forgetting where he came from, where his mother and grandmother still lived, wasn't an option. He'd grown up here, therefore he'd always be invested.

"I know. Still, I want you to know people around here appreciate what you do."

"It's what anyone would do."

"Not everyone. You should go down there and see the work before you leave town."

Kevin didn't go into the small town much when he visited, if at all. He came home to visit family, not to sign autographs and take selfies with fans. But he was curious to see some of the changes that had taken place over the past year or so. "I will."

He'd donated a hundred thousand toward the renovations of the old community center. That's where he'd learned to play basketball and found sanctuary after school until his mother or grandmother got off work. In the years since he'd gone to the league, the town had started to dwindle. He'd given money where he could to support the opening of new businesses and renovate downtown. His donations had paid off. The town was experiencing a surge in regrowth.

Charlotte nodded, obviously pleased with his decision. "Good. Also, before you go, take a look at the old farm across town. I've got a guy interested in buying it. Says he wants to put a drive-in theater over there."

Kevin raised a brow. He shifted sideways on the porch step to look at his grandmother. "A drive-in?"

She nodded. "Yep. Apparently, people like that sort of thing again. The land is just sitting there. Might as well make some money off it."

A thought hit him. Kevin sat up straight. "Grandma C, is the old house still on that land?"

"Not unless it sprouted feet and walked off. Why? That house ain't nothing but ruins now."

Ruins or not, the house might fit a certain sexy photographer's project standards. "Still, if you're selling, we might want to find a way to save it for future generations."

"Boy, you're crazy. How we gonna save my grand-daddy's old cabin?"

With pictures taken by a woman he couldn't wait to see again. He could slap himself for not thinking of this before. He hadn't been to the old farm in years. Had forgotten about the place mostly because Grandma C never mentioned it. Now the old forgotten farm was just what he needed to see Jasmine.

"Don't worry, Grandma C. I know exactly how we're going to save it."

Chapter 5

"Dad says Kathy wants to see us."

Jasmine froze while putting clothes into her suitcase. She jerked her head toward her sister.

Jada sat on the floor with her back against Jasmine's bed. She tossed the yellow stuffed elephant Jasmine had owned since she was five up into the air and caught it on the way down. Her natural hair was pulled up into a curly puff at the top of her head and she had the nerve to look better in the off-white sundress Jasmine had purchased for herself a month ago.

"What? Why would Kathy want to see us now?" Their stepmother hadn't reached out to them in years. After divorcing their father when Jasmine was sixteen, Kathy had moved across country and remarried a year later. She'd had a new life and a new family.

"I don't know. She's divorced again," Jada said flippantly.

The announcement should have elicited some emotion from Jasmine, but the only one that clicked was irritation. Twelve years postdivorce did not endear her to Kathy. "Getting another divorce shouldn't be the reason she suddenly decided to reach out to us. I haven't seen her since I was sixteen. I've moved on."

Jasmine went back to folding clothes to be packed. She would be spending most of the summer down south, documenting homes. Common sense said to travel light because she'd be moving around a lot, but ten years in the fashion industry also meant an extensive wardrobe. Jada was supposed to be helping her separate essentials from nonessentials, not getting her blood pressure up with a conversation about their former stepmother.

Jada spun around on the floor until she faced Jasmine. She held up her hands in a don't-shoot-the-messenger fashion. "Hey, I'm just telling you what Dad said. It's up to you if you see her or not."

"Then the answer is *not*. I don't need to see Kathy and I don't want to." Jasmine held up a bright multicolored skirt she'd picked up in LA last year. The waistband was fitted, accenting her curves, and the hem brushed the floor. "Take or leave?"

"Take," Jada said with a thumbs-up. "You may go to a cookout."

Jasmine raised a brow. "A cookout?"

"It's the South in the summer. If you don't go to someone's cookout, I'm going to be mad at you."

Jasmine laughed, folded the skirt and put it in her bag.

Jada's laughter faded. They were quiet for a few seconds. She stopped tossing the bear. "I'm going to see her."

Jasmine spun around and crossed her arms. "Why?"

"Because she helped raise us. I don't remember Mom, but I remember Kathy. I want to see her."

Jasmine barely remembered their mom. She'd died when Jasmine was five and Jada was two. All she really had were memories of Kathy, too. Followed by the pain of her walking away after the divorce. Kathy made her choice. They weren't her family. Regardless of the memories, Jasmine never had to see her again. "Well, I don't. She's not our mom and she made that perfectly clear."

"Okay, obviously you have some things related to Kathy that you need to work out," Jada said with a hint of attitude. "Talking to her might help."

"Talking to her won't help." She tossed a shirt at Jada. "And I don't have things to work out."

Jada caught the shirt before it hit her in the face. "Sure." She examined the shirt and shrugged. "I'm keeping this now. That's what you get for throwing clothes."

"As if you need a reason to steal my clothes," Jasmine said without heat. Jada had been "borrowing" her clothes for years.

"True. So are you excited about the trip?" Jada rolled up the shirt and put it in her purse sitting next to her on the floor.

"I am. I'm also nervous about what'll happen when I finish. Who really wants to see a bunch of old houses?"

"You're acting as if your pictures won't be beautiful," Jada said, as if people loving Jasmine's work was inevitable. "Or that you won't include the stories of these families. People are going to love it."

Jasmine walked over and sat on the floor next to Jada. "Spoken like my true number one fan."

"Card-carrying member of the Jasmine Hook fan club," Jada said with a finger snap.

Jasmine chuckled and rested her head on her sister's shoulder. Jada was her biggest fan and source of support. She was the only one Jasmine let see her fear of possible failure. The only one she trusted. Jada gave her advice, listened to her vent and laughed when times were good. Jasmine didn't know what she'd do without her sister.

"Keep stealing my dresses," she said, tugging on the dress her sister wore. "And I'm going to revoke your card."

"Nope, that's what comes with the VIP membership."

They both laughed. Jasmine's ringing cell phone interrupted the moment. She lifted her head and shifted to her left in order to pull the phone from her back pocket. The number was unfamiliar, but since she was traveling soon, she didn't want to ignore any unknown calls.

"Hello?"

"Jasmine? It's Kevin."

Her eyes widened. Her heart bucked like a wild stallion. She scrambled off the floor and crossed the room. "Kevin? How did you get my number?"

Jada got up and moved toward Jasmine, curiosity all over her face. She mouthed, "Who is Kevin?"

Jasmine waved her off and went to her bedroom window.

"Rafael gave me your number," Kevin answered.

She was going to kill Rafael. He'd told her she needed to get back in the dating game. He was right about that, but she wasn't sure if Kevin was the right person to jump in with. That didn't stop the excitement pulsing through her veins from his call.

"I didn't expect to hear from you again." She'd figured he would move on after she brushed him off. She had written down his number, and she'd looked at that slip of paper dozens of times in the past two weeks.

"I had to when it became obvious you weren't going to call me."

"I've been busy."

"And I've been thinking about you." His voice was like warm velvet against her skin. Soft, smooth, seductive.

She'd been thinking about him, too. That kiss. How brief it had been. How a guy with baggage wasn't good, not even for short-term flings. "I've sent the pictures of you over to *Sports Fitness* with my recommendation for the cover. Have you seen them yet?"

His low chuckle sent a vibration through her midsection. "You're going to just ignore me saying I've been thinking about you, huh?"

Hell yes. If she didn't, she'd be pulled back into flirting with him. "I'll send the pictures if you haven't seen them."

"I saw them. They're good. Though I don't know which one you suggested for the cover."

"You'll like it." She loved it. A great shot of him jumping with the ball in his hand as he dunked it into the net. Every muscle of his body at play, showcasing the fluid motion he'd accomplished effortlessly. He'd had a smile on his face that showed just how much fun he had playing the game.

"I trust your judgment, then," he said. "Your pictures are actually why I'm calling."

She bit her lower lip and tried to hold back her grin. The compliment about trusting her judgment was simple enough. He should trust her judgment. She was the professional photographer after all. But she'd also had her judgment questioned by subjects a lot over the years. Hearing him say it so effortlessly made her appreciate the words even more.

"The pictures from the photo shoot?"

Jada jumped up onto Jasmine's bed and watched her closely. She waved her hand for Jasmine to come closer and mouthed *who is it?* again. Jasmine put a finger to her mouth.

"No, the pictures for the project you told me about," Kevin said. "Capturing and recording homes owned by freed blacks after the war. I've been thinking about that."

"You have?" Surprise crept into her voice. Sure, he'd seemed interested in her project, but she hadn't expected him to think about it after they parted.

"I know of a place that you might want to capture."

"Where?"

"My family's old farm. My grandma is going to sell the property. I don't see a reason to keep it, but I do think it'll be a good idea to record the history before it's no longer in the family. Will you consider including this in your project?"

Okay, asking her to photograph his family's old property was probably a ploy to see her. But having a property tied to a well-known and well-loved professional athlete wouldn't be a bad thing for the exhibit or the book.

And it's not like you don't want to see the man again.

"I didn't realize you had a family farm."

"I grew up on the land but not in the old house. My grandfather was a farmer. My dad tried his hand at it but was never very good. After he left, my mom and grandmother stopped altogether and got jobs at the local textile mill. When I made it professionally, I moved them both to a new house and haven't looked back." He paused and she heard him grunt. "You didn't ask for all that." He sounded bashful.

"I'm glad you told me all that." Kevin was more than the outgoing ballplayer. His biography said he was born in a small town in South Carolina, but until then, she hadn't pictured him as a Southern boy with country roots. That intrigued her. The urge to know more about him grew.

"Are you interested?"

In a lot more than just taking photos. "Where's the house? I'm going to Georgia this afternoon to meet with Mr. Tatum, the man I told you about who's saving slave cabins. I'll be there for about a week."

"South Carolina in the Pee Dee region. I know that probably means nothing to you. I'll just send you the information," he said. Excitement crept into his hurried reply. She pictured him smiling and her own lips curved. "I'm in town for now, but I've got business in Atlanta and then Jacksonville. I can be back in town to meet you the week after next."

He didn't have to meet her. She could get the information from him, take her pictures without him and get any information on his family via email. On the other hand, talking to him face-to-face and learning what she could from him was the most logical choice.

"I'll think about it," she said while her mind reworked her schedule to include a trip to his place. He didn't need to know how eager she was to see him again. "Let me see how the meeting with Mr. Tatum goes. I may check out some of the places he mentions after we talk. Depending on how long that takes, I'll consider it."

"Does that mean I should look forward to you calling me?"

His cocky, hopeful tone sent heat rising in her cheeks. "I'll call you."

"And will you be thinking about me?"

Damn, how did he do that? Make his voice sound like sex, temptation and a demand all rolled into one? If she weren't going to think about him, which was already doubtful, she'd be dreaming about his voice whispering in her ear anyway.

"I'll be thinking about your family's property," she said.

"And I'll be thinking about that kiss," he countered. "Talk with you soon, Jasmine."

The call ended. Her body tingled everywhere. Everything felt heated, and giddy anticipation made her heart rate flutter. Kevin knew what he was up to. He wanted her, and because their chemistry was undeniable, he wasn't going to let up. She wanted him, too. Couldn't deny that. Not when her body still buzzed from a freaking phone call.

But she didn't want to be an easy catch. Or the dumb girl who fell for the guy she had no business falling for. If he really wanted her, she'd let him court her. Do a little work, while she shored up her defenses. Playboys like Kevin had a knack for breaking down good intentions to keep the heart out of an affair.

"Who is Kevin and why are you looking like you're ready to mail him your panties?" Jada's voice cut into Jasmine's thoughts.

Jasmine spun to her sister and slipped her phone in her back pocket. "No one is mailing anyone their panties."

"Well, you look like he's getting them some way or another." Jada looked up. "Thank the Lord." She focused on Jasmine again. "It's about time you got back out there."

"I never stopped being out there."

"Julio hurt you. Now you're extra cautious. I'm glad to see you're not scared anymore."

Jasmine held up a finger. "First of all, I'm completely over Julio. I ignored the signs that he was still in love with his ex. Second, that's exactly why Kevin isn't a good idea. That was Kevin Koucky with the Jacksonville Gators."

Jada sucked in a breath and put a hand to her chest. "The sexy one with the tats?"

Jasmine rolled her eyes at her sister's antics. "The sexy one with an ex-wife, ex-girlfriend and four kids, who is also photographed with a new flavor every few weeks."

Jada shrugged. "So? You're not trying to marry him, are you?"

Jasmine scoffed and shook her head. "No. I'm trying to focus on my career. This project is what's most important."

"And as a grown-up and mature woman, you can have a little fun with a very sexy man and still stay focused on your career."

"I'm also not trying to get caught up in drama. He's got too much baggage. Combine his baggage with my issues—"

"You don't have issues!" Jada said, clenching her hands into fists as if she wanted to hit something. "Julio was a jackass for making you feel bad about being a juvenile diabetic."

"Agreed, but that doesn't change the fact that any guy who gets with me has to be cool with the idea of needles and 'occasional episodes'—" she made air quotes with her fingers "—when I forget to check my insulin."

Julio couldn't stand dealing with her sickness. He'd walked away whenever she'd pulled out a needle and got angry whenever her blood glucose levels dipped low and she wasn't as coherent. She'd begun to feel bad for being a burden to him when she snapped to her senses and told him to go screw himself. She couldn't help being born with the illness and he either dealt or moved on. A month later, he moved on. Or was that backward, since he reunited with his ex-wife?

Jada waved a finger back and forth. "My point is you don't have to rummage through his baggage any more than he has to know a lot about your illness. Again, you're not trying to marry him."

"I wasn't trying to marry Julio either." The mumbled admission slipped out without a thought.

They'd started as a flirtation. The flirtation had turned into an affair that had lasted for a year. A year! They'd become exclusive. She'd met his kids and his mother. Before she'd know it, she'd fallen in love. Then, boom, he was telling her their relationship wouldn't work because he still loved his ex-wife. She'd seen their wedding photos in *Us Weekly* with the caption "Second Time Is the Best Time."

"Then learn from the past," Jada said easily. "Make Kevin a one-and-done thing. Something to tell your grandkids later."

Jasmine laughed. "I doubt I'll tell my grandkids about my sex life."

"Then something to tell me later. Remember, one and done. Don't let him drag it out into a fake relationship."

Jasmine shook her head and pulled the suitcase off the bed. "I have learned from my past, and the lesson is don't play with fire if you don't want to get burned. Which means I have to be very careful when it comes to this flirtation with Kevin."

Chapter 6

Kevin kept the top down on his Jaguar F-Type as he drove down Silver Springs' historic Main Street. The small town was located close enough to the coast to get a flow of traffic from tourists headed to Myrtle Beach but far enough away to not benefit from tourism money. He took in the changes from the last time he'd come downtown and smiled. The small town was a lot different.

Ten years ago, the shops on Main were closing down, the movie theater was boarded up and there were few restaurants or grocery stores. Seven years ago, he'd invested in a new outlet mall on the outskirts of Silver Springs. The outlet had given tourists a reason to stop on the way to the coast, and the town leaders used that to play up the history of the town and lure people to visit. The plan worked and there were small shops selling local products, quaint bed-and-breakfasts, a new movie theater, the retrofitted center and a brand-new county museum. The town was slowly making its way back up.

He couldn't take credit for the rebound of his hometown, but he was proud of the small part he'd played in the resurgence. His family had roots here. His grandmother could trace their history back to the first families that farmed the area. He didn't want to see those roots completely lost.

The sun was half hidden behind clouds. Enough to make the early-afternoon heat somewhat bearable. He parked in the drive of the Meadow Springs Bed and Breakfast and got out. A noticeable skip in his step. Anticipation hurried his movements as he walked up the stairs to the front door of the renovated colonial-style home. He ran a hand over his freshly cut hair and checked his breath, which was fine, but he pulled a mint out of his pocket and popped it anyway.

Opening the door, he strolled in and smiled at the woman flipping through a magazine behind the counter. She looked up, and her hazel eyes widened. Long braids framed her heart-shaped face and an orange sundress complemented her dark brown skin.

"Kevin! What are you doing here?" Rachel hurried around the counter with her arms held out.

Kevin picked her up and swung her around with a big hug. "I can't come around anymore?"

Rachel slapped his arm and laughed after he put her down. "You're always welcome. Momma is going to be mad she missed you. She and Dad went to Georgetown today. Oh my God, it's great to see you!"

"Likewise." Rachel had been one of his best friends growing up. They'd run through the woods together, searching for hidden treasure, played basketball and kept each other's secrets. She'd been the one to encourage him to talk to Sabrina at the end of eighth grade. He hadn't thought the head cheerleader would be interested in him, and later, Rachel claimed all the credit for their marriage.

She wrapped her hands around one of his and grinned. "How are the kids?"

"They're all great."

He took a few minutes to update her on everything. She thankfully didn't ask about him and Sabrina anymore. Rachel had held out hope they'd one day make their way back to each other. He'd had the same idea when they'd originally divorced. His plan had been to "sow his oats" and settle down later. The settling never happened. Now that he was older, he still cared for Sabrina as the mother of his children and a friend, but knew they wanted different things. She was engaged now, and he was happy for her.

"So, what brings you into town? I know it wasn't just to catch up with me," Rachel said, leaning back against the counter.

Kevin looked at the stairs leading to the rooms, then back at Rachel. "Actually, I'm here to see one of your guests."

Understanding lit his friend's eyes. She grinned mischievously. "Let me guess. The cute woman with blue streaks in her hair and photography equipment."

"She's here?" Excitement crept into his voice. He cleared his throat and tried to look less like a happy puppy waiting to play with its owner.

Rachel saw through him and laughed. "She checked in late yesterday, but she went out this morning and hasn't been back."

"Where did she go?"

"Why are you assuming I keep up with all my guests?" Rachel asked.

"Because you're nosy as hell," he teased.

Rachel patted his arm. "I know, right?" she said with a laugh. "Your girl asked about coffee."

"She's not my girl." The response was automatic. Even though saying so didn't make him feel redeemed or validated. He couldn't get Jasmine out of his mind, and he couldn't wait to see her again. That didn't make her his girl.

"Whatevs," Rachel said with a flip of her wrist. "I sent her down the street to Maryanne's for the best breakfast and coffee in town."

Kevin checked his watch. "How long ago was that?"

"About an hour and a half. She may still be there."

Kevin gave Rachel another quick hug, then walked backward toward the door. "Thanks, Rachel."

Rachel propped a hand on her hip and raised a brow. "Don't let pretty women be the only reason you come through. The summer concert series is going on. Come back on Saturday and take your girl to hear some jazz. You're part of this town. Don't be a stranger."

He didn't intend on being a stranger. His trips home were just always focused on seeing Grandma C and his mom. Not on dealing with the excess attention he often received. He had missed Rachel, though. She'd been in his wedding way back then. She'd also never blamed him or condemned him for the wild few years after his marriage as many of his and Sabrina's other friends had. She'd always supported him.

"I'll do better. I'm in town for a few days. The concert on Saturday sounds like fun."

Rachel clapped and did a hip shimmy. "Good. I'll tell Tank. We'll pack a picnic."

Tank was Rachel's husband. That they were still together all these years later was great. "Sounds good. See both of y'all Saturday."

He waved at Rachel and hurried out the door. Mary-anne's Diner was only a few blocks away. He opted to walk there instead of driving his car the short distance. Long sleeves hid his tattoos. He slipped on a baseball cap that read Little River Zion Church, courtesy of his grandmother. The outfit wouldn't make him totally unrecognizable, but would hopefully keep people from immediately stopping him for autographs and pictures.

He kept his head down as he strolled to the diner. Memories of the old days filled his mind. Hanging out and walking these same streets holding Sabrina's hand. Rachel and Tank with them. Back then, he'd thought he'd known everything. Thought he'd been in love with the girl he'd love forever. That hadn't happened. High school sweetheart love stories like the one Rachel and Tank had were few and far between.

He and Sabrina hadn't wanted the same things. They'd been caught up in teenage emotions that made everything seem larger than life.

He still regretted the way his marriage ended and the years after, when he'd been too busy reveling in the indulgences that came with being a young and famous basketball star to think about anything but the next game, party or adventure. He didn't regret his experiences, but he did regret hurting Sabrina. For being just as selfish as his father had been.

He didn't want to be married. He wasn't made for marriage. His inability to commit to either Sabrina or

Hanna proved that, but Jasmine made him feel a little of those feelings he'd thought was love way back when. He knew better now. He'd never get married again. No commitments and no promises guarded everyone from getting hurt.

When he arrived at Maryanne's, he was surprised to find his high school basketball photo in one of the windows. The words Hometown Hangout of Basketball Star Kevin Koucky were plastered beneath the picture. He chuckled to himself. Dang, that picture was taken forever ago. He was nothing but long limbs, budding muscles and youthful enthusiasm.

He hadn't known anything about disappointments. Hadn't understood the concept that one day his body would break down and force him out of his dream career. He stretched out his hands automatically. The ache was bearable today.

He looked through the glass and quickly spotted Jasmine sitting at the counter, talking to Maryanne, the owner of the diner. They both laughed and looked down at a book on the counter. Forgetting his traitorous joints, Kevin opened the door and entered.

People looked up as they always did when a new person entered but a moment of silence preceded a rush of "Hey, that's Kevin from the Gators!" and "Oh, man, he does hang out here?"

The attention came with the job. He smiled, took pictures and signed a few autographs before telling everyone he was just there for a quick visit and they should enjoy the rest of their breakfast.

When he finally made his way to the counter, Maryanne had a cup of coffee and a stack of pancakes with a side of bacon waiting for him. He'd already eaten at his grandmother's, but no man could resist Maryanne's pancakes.

"You found me," Jasmine said with a sexy upturn of her lips.

He slipped into the chair next to her. She smelled delicious again. A light floral scent that made him want to lean in closer. Her brown eyes were light with pleasure. A navy blue tank top dipped low enough to tease him with a glimpse of soft cleavage, and torn jeans provided more hints of silky brown skin.

"Who said I didn't come for Maryanne's pancakes?" he asked.

"'Cause you haven't come for my pancakes in a few years," Maryanne cut in. "You almost made a liar out of my sign on the window."

He looked at the woman who'd kept him and his friends full on pancakes, burgers and fries throughout high school. There was more gray in her hair and a few more lines around her eyes and mouth, but Maryanne was still full of life and laughter.

"That sign is no lie. I ate here after every basketball game," Kevin replied. "You have just as much responsibility for the state championship as I do."

Maryanne chuckled and drummed her hand on the counter. "That's going up right next to the picture." She tapped the bar and winked. "Good to see you, Kevin. Come around more often. The town misses you."

She strolled away to help another customer. Kevin turned back to Jasmine. "What has she embarrassed me with?"

Jasmine's laugh sent a shot of desire straight through him. She pulled over the book she'd been going through with Maryanne and placed it on the counter between them. "She keeps this old yearbook. There are a lot of pictures of you in here. Even a few of you in this diner."

He looked at the page. Hometown Hangouts was in bold at the top. Various pictures of his classmates at the local places in town filled two pages, a few of him at Maryanne's and other places around town with his teammates and friends.

"Wow, I haven't seen these in forever." He pulled the yearbook closer. "Those were good times." Nostalgia crept into his voice. Memories of those carefree days where life was basketball, high school and having fun.

Jasmine pointed to one of the pictures. Her nails were painted bright green. "That's your ex-wife, right?"

"Yeah, we met in high school. I've known her since… third grade, I think."

"There are a lot of pictures of you two together. You were voted cutest couple."

He'd forgotten about that. He flipped the pages to the one titled Senior Superlatives. "Dang, that was a really ugly shirt. Guess that's why I didn't get Most Fashionable."

She leaned in to look at the picture. "Yeah, that shirt is pretty bad."

Her nearness made the air around him crackle and pop. The dangly star earrings she wore fractured the light, creating rainbows along her neck. He licked his lips, thought about leaning in and kissing her there. His dick tightened. If he didn't think about something else, he'd end up pulling her into his arms in front of everyone. His control, and skills in seduction, were skewed with her so close.

He tried to focus on the picture. The hideous black-and-purple-plaid shirt. "Sabrina used to try to buy me shirts, but I had my own style. I guess I should have listened to her."

"You two were a cute couple." She turned and looked at him.

Her eyes were so brown. She had the longest lashes and the sweetest-looking mouth. Kevin closed the yearbook with one hand. The other ran up her arm. She sucked in a breath and her brown eyes melted like chocolate. "That was a long time ago. And you were right. I was looking for you."

He'd been itching to come find her the second she'd texted she was in town. He hadn't been this into a woman in years. He liked the feeling. He wasn't looking for long-term, but he had missed the feelings of expectation and excitement at the thought of seeing someone. He didn't care what he had to do or how long it took, he was ready to put in the work to get Jasmine in his bed.

She didn't pull back. "I've been walking around downtown." Her voice held a breathless quality that slid and wrapped around him. "The people here credit you for turning things around."

He shook his head. "I didn't do anything."

"You built the outlets that brought in the tourists."

How could she think about the town when all he could focus on was the movement of her lips? The allure of her perfume. How damn happy he was to see her again. "I invested in the place, I didn't build it. The people who live here did that." She opened her mouth to reply, but he ran his thumb over the soft skin in the crook of her elbow. "I didn't come to talk about the town. Come on, let's get out of here."

"Where are we going?"

He was ready to get away from the eyes of the people in the restaurant before he acted on his instincts and kissed her. He didn't need that picture all over the place. "To show you what you came here for," he said.

"I don't have my camera."

"Then we'll stop and pick it up before going to the cabin. Let's go." He hopped out of the chair and stood.

Jasmine pointed to the plate Maryanne had put in front of him. "Aren't you going to eat your pancakes?"

He leaned in close to her ear and whispered, "I'd rather nibble on you."

Her eyes widened. A red tint crept beneath her light brown skin. "Are you saying you're going to bite me?" She didn't sound the least bit offended by the idea.

He leaned one hand on the counter and the other on the backrest of her stool. "Only when you ask me to. Until then, I just plan to dream about kissing you again."

Heat flashed in the depths of her eyes. The edges of her smile lifted, and her breasts rose and fell with her breaths. "Eat your food and then we'll go look at the cabin. That's it."

She tried to sound stern, but her nipples were delightful beacons beneath her shirt and the flush hadn't left her skin. Kevin slowly settled back on the stool. He picked up his fork. "As you wish," he said with a wink.

Delight filled her face. "You watched the movie?"

"When I said I couldn't stop thinking of you, I didn't lie." Which was why he'd watched *The Princess Bride* the day after she'd walked away.

Her smile said she was impressed. Kevin's chest puffed up with the win. Oh yes, he was going to have Jasmine.

Chapter 7

Jasmine snapped another picture of the small home Kevin had brought her to. The original structure only had one room, but Kevin told her other rooms had been added over time. The land around the house was overgrown with grass and weeds. The old fields that sat west of the home were now the beginnings of a young forest.

Kevin stood in front of the house with his back against the faded porch railings. The sun and shadows played over his tall body as if they couldn't resist running across the firm muscles. A fond smile played at his full lips. Jasmine lifted her camera and snapped a picture.

She lowered the camera and took a deep breath. The air was warm, the scent of pine thick. There were no other sounds except for the rustling of the breeze in the trees and the sounds of birds singing.

"It's so peaceful out here," she said. "How long has this land been in your family?"

He blew out a breath and a line formed between his brows. "Let me think. I know my grandfather lived here, and I think he said his dad lived here, too. My grandmother knows more than me. If you want to talk to her, I can introduce you."

A tremble of anxiety shot through her. She quickly squashed the reaction. Meeting his grandmother had nothing to do with them and everything to do with her project. "That sounds good. If you think she'll talk to me."

His answering smile made her heart jump. "She'll talk to you. My grandma loves to talk about the family."

He pushed away from the porch and strolled toward the back of the house. Jasmine followed. "Tell me what you know."

"I know that we used to grow corn over there." He pointed to the overgrown area to the left. "And peanuts, too. We'd sell the peanuts and some of the corn. My granddad wasn't a big farmer. Just grew enough for the family to eat and sell a little. He also worked at the textile mill."

"Did you live with them?"

"My mom stayed over there." They were at the back of the house and he pointed to an area that wasn't as overgrown. "She and my dad had a trailer on that spot. I was at my grandparents' a lot. When I bought Mom and Grandma a new house, she sold the trailer."

"Where's your dad?"

He shrugged. "I don't know. My parents split when I was eleven. He left quickly after. He hated it here. Thought the town was too small." Kevin bent over and snapped off a tall blade of grass. He twisted it and tossed the pieces on the ground. "Last I heard, he married someone else and had a new family. He tried to contact me once, right after I was drafted. I quickly told him to leave me the hell alone."

There was no pain in his voice. That didn't mean the pain wasn't there. She'd gotten good at hiding how much it hurt when Kathy had walked out of her life.

"Some people don't like the quiet," she said. "They have too much time to think about things. Some choose to focus on what they don't have instead of their blessings. That's their problem."

"I understand that now," Kevin replied. "I like silence. I can clear my head of all the bad. That's why I come home every off-season. I don't really go into town, but I hang with my grandma and mom. Eat too much food, listen to the latest town gossip and chill before getting back to the grind."

Silver Springs was vastly different from the city Jasmine had grown up in outside of Richmond, Virginia. She'd lived in New York since graduating college. She liked the hustle and bustle of the city, but she could appreciate the silence of the country, as well—appreciated that Kevin still looked at his home as a place of solace instead of someplace to run away from and forget.

Jasmine picked a yellow dandelion and tucked it behind her ear. "The people here love you."

"That's just because I'm a basketball star." He walked over to one of the trees where an old rope and tire swing hung.

"No, they love you because you give back. You've done a lot for this town."

Kevin tugged on the rope. His biceps bulged quite nicely with the movement. "I only do what I can to keep the town alive. My family is here. I don't want them to be in a place that's stagnant."

"Sounds like you've supported smart moves to make the town prosper." She went over to him. Snapped a few pictures of him testing the tree and swing.

Lines formed around his mouth as he slowly uncurled his hands from around the rope. "I've been lucky with my picks of things to invest in."

"Do you invest in other places or just here?"

"Other places and other businesses. I know that all it takes is one injury. One illness—" he looked at his hands "—and I'm out of the game. Early on, I listened to the older players and invested my money to have multiple streams of income."

"I told you you were smart," she said with a grin.

"Yeah, but I didn't invest because I thought that it'd be my whole long-term plan." He ran a hand over the curve of the tire. "I have no idea what I'll do if I retire." He looked and sounded lost and frustrated. The smile was gone, along with the normally ever-present spark in his eye.

Jasmine skipped over to him. She placed her hand over his on the tire swing, forcing his attention off thoughts of an uncertain future. "What's something you love doing now?"

The spark returned and he flashed a cocky grin. "You really want to ask me that?"

A flutter started low in her stomach. That's what she got for trying to bring his smile back. "In a nonsexual way. What do you like to do?"

He considered her words. "I really don't know. Basketball is all I've done for so long. I'll have to get back to you on that." He focused on her. "What about you? Tell me about your family."

"What? Why?" She wasn't prepared for the question.

Kevin moved until he stood behind her. Strong hands rested on her hips. "Because I want to get to know you." His voice was a warm caress in her ear. The flutter in her stomach intensified and heat spread between her thighs.

"There's nothing to know," she said, trying to keep her voice steady. "I'm very boring."

One hand lifted and flipped her blue-tipped bangs. "You're definitely not boring."

Soft lips brushed her ear before he pulled away. She swayed on her feet, her heart pounding and need growing inside. Damn, he was too good at making her want more of his touch.

"You're just trying to flatter me."

"That, too," he said with a grin. "But I really am curious."

She pushed the tire swing. Watched it sway instead of looking at him. "My mom died when I was five. I don't really remember her. My dad remarried when I was seven. Then he and my stepmom divorced when I was sixteen. I have one sister and she's my best friend."

"Do you still talk to your stepmom?"

"No." More heat than she'd intended crept into her voice. She glanced at Kevin to see if he'd noticed.

He raised a brow but didn't question anymore. Relief rushed through her. He slipped the phone from his pocket. "My turn."

"To do what?" she asked hesitantly.

"To take your picture." He tapped the screen, then held the phone up with the camera facing her.

Jasmine laughed and held up a hand. She backed up a few steps. "Oh no. I don't take pictures."

"You've got to be kidding me. A photographer that doesn't like to take pictures?"

"I photograph beautiful things and people. I don't photograph me." She turned away.

Kevin's hand was on her shoulder before she could walk far. He pulled her back against his front and held up the phone. The camera on selfie mode. He leaned down until his head was next to hers. "You're a beautiful person." He snapped the picture.

She sank into the warmth of his embrace. She could enjoy being held by him for a few seconds longer. "You're a flirt." She knew she was cute, but she wasn't beautiful. She was fun, quirky and outgoing. That more than made up for not having movie-star good looks. But it didn't mean she liked taking pictures of herself. She hated herself on camera.

"I tell the truth." He snapped another selfie. Then kissed her cheek. Her eyes widened and he snapped that picture. Jasmine laughed at his antics and he snapped several more.

She spun around to face him. "You're ridiculous." The words didn't carry any heat.

"If I ever hear you refer to yourself as not beautiful enough to be photographed, I'm going to toss you over my knee and spank you."

She raised a brow. "Into the kinky, are we?"

His full lips lifted and her world became brighter. "I'm into anything when it comes to you."

He wrapped an arm around her waist and pulled her forward. His head lowered and he kissed her. Not a brief brush like before, but a full-fledged kiss. His lips were firm but gentle against hers, her reasons for needing to stay away from Kevin forgotten. She was an adult.

She knew this wasn't forever. There was no reason to deny their attraction.

Her tongue slid across his lower lip. Kevin let out a soft moan and opened to her. She lost herself in the kiss. His mouth on hers was still soft and sensual, but his kiss went deeper, a little darker. The pulse of power in his large body was even more pronounced now that she was pressed against him. Her camera between them kept her from getting closer. For once in her life, she considered throwing the thing to the side.

He pulled back slowly. "Would you like to see more places around here?"

She blinked several times. "What?"

"I'm thinking of cabins."

She laughed and pushed away from him. She deserved that, but the fire in his eye and the feel of his mouth against hers still tingling on her lips meant she didn't care. "Yes. I would like to see more cabins."

Noon had come and gone by the time Jasmine and Kevin made it back to the bed-and-breakfast. He'd taken her to three other places, all from families he'd known growing up in the area. Jasmine had been pleased to learn Silver Springs had started out as a sort of haven for free blacks during the Reconstruction, grew as a farming town and boomed even more in the thirties with the opening of a textile mill.

Many of the families he knew had been there since the area was officially incorporated as a town in 1920. Jasmine's brain was already racing with the idea of documenting the old homes and talking to the members of the founding families. The place and town would have been all but forgotten if Kevin hadn't stepped in with investments to help his hometown prosper when industry moved out.

"Thank you for the tour," she told him as they walked up the stairs into Meadow Springs. "There's so much history here. I'll probably be in town a lot longer than I planned."

Kevin placed his hand on the small of her back, the steady pressure of his touch a pleasant feeling. "I don't have any complaints with that."

"How long are you going to be in town?" She supposed he had other things he did in the off-season besides hang out here.

"I've got a few meetings here and there but mostly visits planned with my kids and a quick vacation with friends early next month." He opened the door for her. "I'll be around for at least another two weeks."

Two weeks and then he would be gone. She was on no specific deadline for this project. She had several months before she was scheduled to exhibit at the gallery and could spend as much time in Silver Springs as she liked. The idea of him not being there if she chose to be in town longer than two weeks took some of the shine off her excitement.

"I know you want to spend time with your family and friends in town, so don't feel as if you have to escort me every day." She entered the cool interior and breathed a sigh of relief. She hadn't realized how much the temperature had risen until the air-conditioning hit her.

"I can catch up with friends and help you out. You said tomorrow you'll start reaching out to some of the families. Since I know a few, I'll put in a good word for you. Let them know you're not some raving lunatic."

She laughed and looked up at him. There were so few guys she was able to look up at. Most were eye level or shorter when she wore heels. Today she'd traded in her boots for casual sneakers. Kevin's height and muscle made her feel tiny in comparison, but also sheltered and protected instead of threatened. Even though she didn't need protection, she liked the feeling.

"Hey, Kevin, look who came to see you," Rachel said from behind the counter.

Jasmine had liked Rachel when she'd chatted with her briefly this morning. The woman was friendly and helpful. Now she and a tall man who was slim except for a slightly rounded stomach both grinned at Kevin.

Kevin's face lit up with surprise and recognition. "Tank?"

Tank laughed as he crossed the room and gave Kevin a hug. "Nobody has called me Tank in years."

The two men embraced and slapped each other on the back. "Oh yeah, it's Coach Givens now," Kevin said. "You're doing big things."

"Not compared to you, but I'm trying," Tank said.

Kevin shook his head. "Taking the high school team to the regional finals is big things. That hasn't happened since we played. Good job, Tank."

Tank rubbed his chin and grinned self-consciously. "I got a good group of kids this year. Thank you for the donation to renovate the gym. That really gave the team a sense of pride they needed. It's translated on and off the court."

"Hey, man, no thanks required. Just take them to the playoffs again and I'm repaid." Kevin shifted toward Jasmine. He placed his hand on her lower back and brought her forward. "Tank, this is Jasmine Hook. Photographer extraordinaire to the Hollywood rich and famous. Jasmine, this was the best team captain the Silver Springs Saints ever saw."

Jasmine smiled and shook his hand. "Nice to meet you, Tank."

"Same here." He eyed her with curiosity and threw a look Kevin's way.

"Jasmine is documenting the old homes of blacks during and after the Reconstruction," Kevin said. "She's got a book deal and a New York gallery exhibit lined up to display the photos. I took her out to your great-grandparents' old place." He looked at Jasmine. "That was the last one we visited."

Jasmine swung her head in Tank's direction. The quick movement made her head spin. "Oh, I'd love to talk to you more about that. Get some history of your family, if you don't mind." Her tongue felt like a thick tube sock in her mouth, making the words come out slower than she'd expected.

"Do I mind? Not at all. My family helped found this town, but after the textile mills came in, they swept our contributions under the rug. I'd love to set the record straight."

Jasmine smiled her thanks, but her vision began to tilt. She'd pushed too hard today and now she was about to pay for it.

Kevin, Tank and Rachel talked about other families and places she could photograph. All good information, but the trembles started. First in her hands before slowly taking over her body. A cold, clammy sweat coated her like slime and nausea churned.

"Excuse me a second. I need to grab something in my room," she said. She turned away and focused on getting one foot in front of the other as she made her way to the stairs. Her room was on the second floor. Not far from the top of the stairs. She should be able to make it okay.

She stumbled on the first step. A strong arm wrapped around her waist. Kevin's body supported her weight.

"Hold on. I've got you." His voice was warm and steady.

She hated appearing weak in front of him, but the room spun more with each passing second. "First door on the right. Keys are in my pocket."

He helped her up the stairs, dug the keys out and got her inside. Jasmine pointed to the bathroom. "There's a black case on the counter. Bring it please."

He quickly retrieved it and brought it back to her. "What's going on?"

"I pushed too hard," she said, taking the case from him. "My blood sugar is probably low."

Not probably. Definitely. She only got this woozy, sick feeling when her levels dropped. She opened the case and pulled out the glucose meter.

Kevin knelt on the floor next to her. He didn't say anything, just watched her closely as she checked her blood. He didn't look away, nor cringe at the sight of it. She'd commend him if she wasn't feeling like she'd gone for a hundred twirls on a merry-go-round.

The reading was abysmal. She should have taken her meter with her, but when he'd asked her to go, she'd been so excited about getting started and then had enjoyed his company so much common sense slipped.

With a lifetime of practice, she took out the needle and prepared an insulin shot. The pressure of his hand didn't go away while she worked. He looked worried and nervous. She felt bare and self-conscious as he watched her. She wasn't embarrassed—juvenile diabetes was a part of her life she couldn't hide—but he watched her so intently. With concern instead of the distaste Julio had shown. She needed space.

"Can you get me a juice from the cooler over there?" She used her chin to indicate a cooler next to the bed.

He was instantly up on his feet and across the room. Jasmine injected the insulin while he was distracted. When he came back, she was pulling her shirt down over her side and sitting up straight.

"Capri Sun?" he asked with a raised brow.

"Hey, it works," she replied and reached for the juice.

He inserted the straw into the foil packet before handing it to her, then knelt on the floor next to her again. "What happened?"

She sipped the sweet juice before putting the needle away in her case and closing it. She'd safely dispose of it later. "I didn't plan to be out for so long. It was hot and I did a lot of moving around. Usually I keep my case with me or at least some snacks so my levels don't tank."

Kevin ran a hand over his face. His expression grim. "Shit, this is my fault. I shouldn't have kept you out so long."

"No, I've been diabetic all my life. I know better. I was having fun and got caught up in the work. It's happened before. It's not your fault."

"I still feel terrible."

She wrapped her hand around his on the arm of the chair. "Don't. You gave me a lot to work with. And even though I'm embarrassed, thanks for being my shoulder to lean on."

He studied her with worried eyes. "Don't be embarrassed. When you stumbled. I haven't been that worried in a long time."

"It looks scarier than it is," she said to try to make him feel better. "I'll do better tomorrow. It's just that my brain and body don't always sync up. I think I can push forever, and my body reminds me it's not invincible."

His face said he could relate. "That is a hard pill to swallow. Your body not doing what your brain still thinks it can do."

"You have no idea."

His sigh was full of defeat. "You'd be surprised." Before she could ask what that was about, he leaned up and kissed her on the forehead. His lips were dry and warm against her still clammy skin. He didn't pull back quickly, instead keeping his lips against her for a few seconds and taking a deep breath as if breathing her in. "Get some rest, Jasmine." When he pulled back, his eyes were tender. "I'll check on you later."

"I'll be fine."

"That doesn't mean I won't check on you." Then his cocky smile came out and made her world tilt again for other reasons. "I'm trying to seduce you and it's not fair to do so when you're swooning for other reasons."

She rolled her eyes and laughed. Fatigue slowly seeping in to replace the woozy feeling. "You are crazy."

"Yeah, crazy about a photographer with hidden tattoos and blue streaks in her hair." He stood, then leaned over to press another kiss to her ear. "I can't wait to find out if you have other tattoos."

Her pulse jumped. She clenched her thighs together

as delicious tingles traveled over her sex. "I've got a few and hidden piercings, too." And there went her low blood sugar loss of a filter. Jada often said Jasmine needed to watch what she said when her blood glucose levels tanked.

Kevin groaned and nipped her ear. "No fair to say that when you're sick." He straightened.

A noticeable bulge was in the front of his pants. Jasmine's breathing hitched and she bit her lower lip. "I'm not sick." That point was arguable, but right now her tired brain couldn't focus on anything except how absolutely delicious his lips looked.

"Don't tempt me, Jasmine." He backed toward the door. "I'll see you in the morning."

The door closed firmly behind him. Jasmine watched it and held her breath. Hoping for him to come back and knowing she really needed to get rest. When she finally had to breathe, she let it out in a rush. She appreciated him being noble and taking the higher ground. She had nearly fallen up the stairs. As only she could do in epic fashion. Of course he wouldn't stay and throw her in bed the way she wanted him to.

She moved to get up and crawl into bed. The door opened again suddenly. Kevin strode to her with quick steps. He lowered to his knees in front of her, took her face in his hands and kissed her. Slowly, deeply and oh so thoroughly. Her breasts ached, and the tightness between her thighs grew to a fever pitch.

When he pulled back, his breathing was ragged. "Sorry, but the thoughts of hidden tattoos is going to keep me up all night. I'm an asshole, because I want you up all night, too." He stood and went to the door. He turned the knob. "Until tomorrow, Jasmine." He left.

"Asshole," she said with a smile on her face. She'd be up all night now, too.

Chapter 8

Every day, Kevin looked forward to seeing Jasmine and taking her around town. By the end of the week, he was downright giddy. A new experience for him. He hadn't been giddy to meet up with a woman since he was fourteen.

They'd spent the week going around talking to some of the family members connected to the locations she'd photographed. He didn't have to go with her. Word of her presence had spread with the lightning-fast speed of all news in a small town. But he'd enjoyed catching up with people he hadn't seen in years and hearing the stories he'd grown up with, all while Jasmine smiled enthusiastically.

Kevin hurried getting dressed and into the kitchen for juice to wash down the prescriptions his doctor had given him for the joint pain. The meeting with his agent was coming up in a few weeks. He had to make a decision about the next season. He wasn't looking forward to it.

Grandma C was in the kitchen already. She had a cup of coffee and a cinnamon roll in front of her while she read the morning paper, a daily ritual she refused to give up. Kevin had gotten her and his mom a computer and a laptop, but his grandma insisted on reading her news the old way.

"Morning, Grandma C." He strolled over and kissed her forehead.

"I see you're up and eager to go meet that girl again," she said with a sparkle in her eye.

"I'm just helping her out with a project. That's all." He went to the fridge and pulled out a carton of orange juice.

"Mmm-hmm, then why haven't you brought her over here for me to talk to yet? I know she's been talking to some of the other families in the area after taking pictures of their old land."

Kevin had been sincere when he'd made the offer for Jasmine to talk to his grandmother about their family property. Her meeting his grandmother in that sense wasn't a big deal, but somehow it also felt like the biggest of deals.

He hadn't brought any woman around to meet his family since Hanna, and that was because she'd gotten pregnant. Hanna lived in California, and their relationship, though long-term, had been a long-distance one with no expectations of it becoming serious enough for her to meet his family. He and Jasmine weren't together, but they were getting close.

He hadn't pushed her toward taking their situation past the few quick and hot kisses they'd shared. He liked her, got the sense she liked him, and she definitely liked his kisses if her soft moans were any indication. But she hadn't invited him back into her room, he couldn't bring her back here, and he didn't want to be crass enough to book a hotel room in town. So he waited.

"I'll bring her over this weekend," he answered after swallowing his medicine.

"Your mom is coming back this weekend. She may bring the twins with her," Charlotte said, flipping a page of the paper.

"Yeah, I talked to her and the twins last night. They like coming to visit."

"I like having them here," she said with a smile. "Does this mean you're going to introduce your girl to the twins?"

Kevin laughed at his grandmother's insistence on making this thing with Jasmine into something bigger. If his laugh sounded a little tight and anxious, he ignored it. He wasn't starting something serious with Jasmine. They were getting to know each other. Having fun. Hopefully sleeping together soon.

"Mom said they'll be in late Sunday evening. I'll bring Jasmine by earlier in the day."

"Why not bring her Saturday?"

"The summer concert is Saturday. I'm taking her there."

Charlotte's eyes widened. "A date?"

"To hang with Rachel and Tank and get more of an idea of the flavor of the town."

"You've got a lot of excuses."

"And you're trying really hard to turn nothing into something. We're cool, Grandma. I like Jasmine, and yes, she's attractive, but nothing serious is coming out of this. I'm done with serious relationships." He put the orange juice away and checked his watch.

"I can still pray that you'll find peace." She sipped her coffee and looked at the paper.

"I've found peace. My kids are doing well. I've got good relationships with their mothers, and you and Mom are comfortable."

"Then why are you afraid of love?"

"I'm not afraid," he said quickly. He just didn't believe it was in him to really love deeply. Maybe his dad had left him something after all.

"See, not peaceful. And," she continued when he was about to cut in, "you'd still rather take pain medicine than face what's going on with your body. Not peaceful. You need to accept what's happening instead of fighting everything that goes against what you planned."

Kevin gritted his teeth. His grandmother's frank words cut deeper than he wanted to face. Deeper than he wanted to feel. Instead of arguing with her, something he wouldn't win anyway, he walked over and kissed her forehead again.

"I'll be back in a few hours. Call me if you need anything."

She patted his back and shook her head. "I'm going to meet Cindy at that new bakery around lunchtime. She said their red velvet cake is almost as good as mine," Charlotte grunted. "As if that would ever happen."

Kevin released a breath and a prayer of thanks. She wasn't going to insist on digging deeper than he wanted to this early in the morning. This early in his life. "She had to have hit her head. No one makes red velvet as good as you." He picked up his keys and went to the back door.

"Have fun with your girl, Kevin. Can't wait to meet her."

Kevin smiled grimly and left the house. One week, and then he'd be out of town. He'd meet with his agent and give him the bad news. At the ripe old age of thirty-six, Kevin Koucky was retiring due to a rheumatoid arthritis diagnosis. He was done, useless, and had no clue what to do next. Who would he be without suiting up in his jersey at the start of the season?

Kevin pushed aside the unsettling thoughts of the coming week and instead focused on what was coming. He was meeting up with Jasmine. This was his last week with her and then he wouldn't see her again.

The uneasy feeling in his gut intensified. He wasn't ready for their time to end, and not because he hadn't slept with her yet.

Short-term was better anyway, he thought as he slipped behind the wheel of his car. He didn't want to see the look of disappointment in her eyes when she realized his body was breaking down. When she realized he was useless.

Chapter 9

Jasmine was just slipping on her earrings when there was a knock on her door. She did one last check on herself in the mirror and was pleased with the results. Packing the colorful skirt had been smart. She hadn't made it to a cookout, but Kevin asking her to go with him to the summer concert series was just as good a reason in her book. She'd paired the skirt with a fitted white tank and dressed the outfit up a little with large white earrings and a matching shell necklace.

She hurried to the door, nerves and eagerness speeding her steps. Stopping short of reaching for the knob, she took a deep breath and centered herself.

Tonight was the night. No more fighting herself and playing cat and mouse with Kevin. He was only in town for another week. After that, she'd never see him again. She was going to invite him up.

Swinging the door open, Jasmine's breath stuck in her throat. Kevin was on the other side, as expected, but what wasn't expected was the huge bouquet of brightly colored flowers in his hand. He'd dressed casually in white linen pants and a light blue button-up that fitted his muscled body just enough to make her mouth water.

"Those are beautiful," she said, eyeing the flowers but really thinking about the width of his shoulders and taut flatness of his abdomen.

He held the bouquet out to her. "I may not live here permanently, but I'm still a Southern gentleman. My grandmother would skin me if I didn't bring flowers to my date."

Jasmine chuckled and took the flowers from him, her heart skipping a little at the mention of this being a date. The sweet fragrance wrapped around her the way she wanted Kevin's arms to embrace her. "Is your grandmother the only reason I got flowers?" she teased.

She turned and took the flowers over to the dresser. There wasn't a vase in the room, but there was a vanity pitcher and bowl on the dresser. She grabbed the pitcher and put the flowers inside, setting it next to her bed.

"That, and when I saw them, I thought of you. Bright, colorful, happy." He watched her from the door, one shoulder leaned against the jamb. Since that day she'd gotten sick and he'd helped her, he hadn't crossed the threshold. She appreciated him respecting her space but really wished he'd cross into it and kiss her again.

She grabbed her clutch purse and strolled back over to him. "You should have led with that."

He straightened and slipped a hand over her waist. "How about I lead with this instead?" He lowered his lips over hers.

The kiss was quick and hot and her body burned with need instantly. She placed her hands on the solid firmness of his chest. Eased up on her toes to get closer. Kevin deepened the kiss. His hand on her waist tightened and he pulled her closer. The rise of his desire between them made her knees melt like butter. Oh yes, she couldn't hold out anymore. She was just about to pull back and suggest they skip the concert when Kevin broke the kiss and eased away.

His nostrils flared with his heavy breaths. He licked his lower lip and took a step back. "We better get moving before Rachel and Tank come looking for us."

Yes. Rachel and her husband. They were meeting them. The fun times could come later. "Yes, let's do that."

She locked her room. Kevin offered her his arm and led her downstairs.

The summer concert was being held in the town square. Since the area wasn't far, she and Kevin chose to walk the short distance. The night was warm, the slightly humid air broken by a soft breeze that made the weather pleasant. On the way there, Kevin pointed out places around town where he'd played with friends, fallen on his bicycle and scraped his knees or just hung out, the stories weaving a tale of a happy kid who loved roaming and exploring his small town.

"This place was all I knew," he said as they entered the square. "Imagine the culture shock when I was drafted. Suddenly, my world went from this town and everyone knowing my family to the bright lights and whirlwind of being a celebrity."

"That had to have been overwhelming."

"I wish there were a word bigger than that. I wasn't ready for being famous. I thought I was, but I don't think anyone is really ready. Suddenly everyone knew my name, people I'd never met were excited to talk to me and anything I could think to ask for I was able to get. That was a heady experience. I loved it."

"You don't anymore?"

People waved and greeted them as they walked through the square. A good many had come out. The sounds of contemporary jazz drifted in the air from the small stage. A few couples danced along to the music.

Kevin spotted Rachel and Tank. He waved, then headed in their direction. "No, I don't," he answered as they walked to his friends. "I love basketball. I love the friends I made. I love being surrounded by guys who love the game as much as me, but I'm no longer blinded by the people wanting a piece of me. I learned my lesson."

She didn't get to ask how he'd learned the lesson because they were joining Rachel and Tank. She'd save that for later. If there was a later. She only had one more week with Kevin. If she was really going to keep this casual, then deep questions about what emotional scars he carried didn't belong in the conversation.

"You got here just in time," Rachel said. "Tank's nephew is playing. He's got the keyboard solo in the next song."

Tank pointed to two extra folding chairs they'd brought, and Jasmine and Kevin settled in. The conversation flowed again around old times and the musicians. When Rachel and Tank got up to dance, Kevin took Jasmine's hand and pulled her to join the rest of the couples in front of the stage. They danced and laughed when Kevin stepped on her toes.

"I never claimed to be a good dancer."

"I'll remember that before ever dancing with you again," she joked.

He twirled her and she laughed. They switched off and Rachel danced with Kevin while Jasmine danced with Tank. The night was fun, the music great and even though it was obvious the people in town were excited that Kevin was there, he wasn't swarmed by those in attendance, though they were interrupted a few times for selfie and autograph requests.

"Let me show you something," Kevin said after signing an autograph for one of his fans.

"What?"

He took her hand. "Rachel, Tank, we're going to head out."

Rachel threw him a curious look. Tank grinned and shook Kevin's hand. "It was fun hanging out."

"It was," Kevin said. "I'll give you both a call before I leave next week. We'll hang out again."

"I'm holding you to that," Rachel said. She jumped up and hugged Kevin.

After saying goodbye, Kevin led her out of the park. "The concert isn't over." Jasmine said.

"I know. I was ready to get out of there. Most people respected our space, but I noticed the autograph requests were picking up. Better to leave before things get crazy."

She nodded but couldn't add anything. She didn't mind leaving. She'd been having a good time but was ready to be alone with him.

"So what are you showing me?"

His eyes twinkled with a devilish spark. "The kissing tree."

Jasmine laughed. "The what?"

He took her across the street to one of the small parks

next to the city hall. The music from the concert could still be heard, but it was fainter. The park was deserted, most of the town in the square for the concert. Kevin pointed to the large magnolia in the center.

"That is the kissing tree." He headed in that direction. "There was always a festival or something in the square. If you really liked a girl and wanted to kiss her without someone seeing, there aren't many places downtown. But if you come over here and go on the backside of the tree—" which he did "—then no one could see you on the other side of the street in the square."

"Are you serious? Wouldn't the parents see all of the kids coming over here and wonder what was up?"

"Good point. Okay, busted. I just wanted to be alone with you and since you haven't invited me to your room…" He pulled her into his arms. "I didn't need the entire town to see me when I kissed you again."

Jasmine wrapped her arms around his neck. "You can kiss me here." She lifted up on her toes. "Or you can kiss me in my room."

Kevin's body stilled. "Are you serious?"

"We've only got a week. Let's stop playing around."

Kevin's eyes flared so hot she was surprised the magnolia didn't catch fire. "I couldn't agree more. Except I'm spoiled. I want both."

His head lowered and his lips brushed hers. Jasmine had no complaints. Kissing him again before going to her room seemed like an excellent idea.

The sound of glass breaking followed by yelling interrupted them. They broke apart quickly, confusion in both their eyes.

"That didn't sound good," Jasmine said.

They hurried around the magnolia just in time to

see a group of teens around a car. One teen reached in and took something.

"Hey!" Kevin yelled.

The kids jumped as one. The group eyed Kevin and Jasmine like frightened gazelles caught by an alligator's gaze, then turned and fled.

Kevin's cell phone rang. "Damn, just a second." He pulled out his phone and frowned. "It's Tank." He answered the call. "Tank, what's up?"

In the relative quiet of the park, she could hear a little bit of Tank's voice. Kevin listened, then cursed. "Yeah, I think I know who did it. I just saw a group of kids break into a car. Give me a second to get Jasmine back, then I'll be right there."

"What's wrong?" Jasmine asked after Kevin ended the call.

"Tank's windows are busted, too."

"What the hell?" Jasmine looked in the direction the kids had fled.

"Yeah, I know. It's not just his car. A few others on the street where he parked. He says there are some teens that have been causing problems."

"I thought Silver Springs was perfect."

He shook his head. "Every town has its troublemakers. I'll go help him. Then—" he lifted her hand and kissed the back of it "—I'll come see you."

"Do you want me to come, too? I saw the kids, as well. I can help identify them."

He shook his head. "No. I thought I recognized one. A kid of one of my former friends." He sighed and ran a hand over his face. "If it is, this won't be fun. Let me help Tank and talk to the police, then I'll be right back."

She nodded. If he recognized one of the kids, then

his identification would be better than hers. "But if they need me to say anything, let me know."

"I will."

He took her back to Meadow Springs. She waved as he drove away to help his friend, then hurried upstairs.

She hated the fact that a few delinquent teens were breaking into cars. Though Kevin said he'd be back soon, she doubted he'd be back within an hour. She'd take the time to shower and get ready for him to return. The night wasn't overly hot, but it was humid enough to make her sweat.

She showered and put on a pink lacy camisole and shorts set. That was the only sexy set of pajamas she'd brought on this trip. Fun times hadn't been on the original agenda. She put lotion on and lay on the bed to wait. And wait. And wait some more.

Kevin texted two hours later. Still at police station. Should be done soon.

Sighing, Jasmine tossed the phone on the pillow next to her and stared at the ceiling. Her was body both exhausted from the long day and tight with anticipation. She'd fallen asleep when her ringing cell woke her up another two hours after the text.

"Kevin?" she answered groggily.

"Sorry, this thing with the kids is taking longer than I thought." He sounded tired. "They found the kids. One of them is the one I recognized. He plays on Tank's team. He's a good kid hanging with the wrong crowd. We're trying to work with the cops to not throw the book at the boys. I won't make it by tonight."

The disappointment in his voice matched the heavy feeling in her chest. She glanced at the clock. It was past midnight. She could still ask him over, but that officially put her in "booty call" territory. She and Kevin may not be forever, but that didn't mean she wanted their first time to be a post-midnight drop-in after he'd left the police station. The romantic mood of earlier was effectively killed.

"No, I understand," she said, trying to sound relaxed when her body still yearned for his touch. "You helping where you can is most important."

"I'm really sorry about this."

"Don't be. You're a good guy. That's sexy."

He chuckled. "I'll remember that. Good night, Jasmine. I'll pick you up tomorrow and we can talk with my grandmother."

"See you then. Good night, Kevin."

She ended the call and let out a disappointed, frustrated breath.

Chapter 10

Watching Jasmine's eyes light up as his grandmother told stories about their family was something Kevin doubted he'd ever tire of. They were on the back porch. The late-afternoon sun formed shadows around the edges of the yard. A cool breeze along with the ceiling fans on the porch ceiling made the evening pleasant. Jasmine and his grandmother sat at the glass table on the right side of the porch. He sat in his favorite spot on the step.

He'd heard this story about his great-grandfather before, but seeing Jasmine's interest made it seem new. She leaned toward Charlotte, her eyes wide and her body alert with anticipation. He lifted his cell phone and captured the picture. He still took pictures with her and snapped a few of his own candid shots. Jasmine was beautiful, and her personality made her radiant. Her not liking the way she looked in pictures made no sense to him.

"What happened after that?" Jasmine asked, leaning closer to his grandmother.

Charlotte's eyes were bright. Her joy from having an enthusiastic audience was written all over her face. "I was little, so the adults didn't tell me everything. We were all asleep that night when someone banged on the door. I tried to look out the window, but my mom pulled me back. I could still see the flicker of the flames. The men dragged my dad off."

"What did they do to him?"

Charlotte's eyes turned sad. "No one ever told me. Mom got a call the next morning from someone telling her where to pick up my dad. My uncles went and got him, brought him home. They rushed him into the bedroom before I could see him, but I sneaked and looked. He was beat up pretty bad." She got a faraway look. Lost in the past and a tragic memory. "Daddy never did go back to work at the mill after that. The guys stopped their protests to get paid what they were due. Things got hard after that. Mom started working in town, cleaning houses for the wives of the plant supervisors. Daddy worked the farm. He was different after that. Meaner. Momma said it was the only way he knew how to be a man again after they came and got him."

His grandmother's eyes were sad. She shook her head and blinked a few times. "Sometimes he was still nice to me. Not often, but sometimes I saw the man he used to be."

Jasmine reached over and placed her hand over Charlotte's. "Can I tell your father's story?"

"You want to tell his story? Do you think people will care?"

"Your father was a happy, proud and strong man. All

he wanted to do was get equal pay for the guys working at the mill and he was punished for it. His work on your farm kept your land in your family and helped provide a home for Kevin and his mother. His story deserves to be told."

Charlotte smiled and placed her hand over Jasmine's. Kevin thought he saw the glint of tears in her eyes. He had to look away as his own eyes burned.

He'd heard the story. Knew that his great-grandfather had been humiliated and beaten until there was nothing left but bitterness and anger. His grandmother and mother hadn't had things easy. That's why he worked so hard to give back and make their lives easier now. His family's story was nothing special, but the idea that Jasmine wanted to tell it anyway cemented his need to be with her.

A few nights for a week wasn't enough. He wanted her as a long-term lover. Yes, he'd failed at two long-term relationships already, but if they both entered this knowing they would eventually call things to an end, maybe it could work out.

The challenge was figuring out how to get her to agree to that before he left town in a few days. Last night when she'd invited him to her room, she'd said they didn't have a lot of time. Meaning she probably only wanted a quick fling. He needed to convince her to at least give him the summer before he left for Jacksonville.

"Yes," Charlotte said with a firm nod. "You can tell my daddy's story."

Jasmine smiled. "Thank you."

His grandmother blinked several times. "You know

what? I better go check on that peach cobbler I've got in the oven." She stood.

"You need any help, Grandma C?" Kevin asked.

She waved him away and for once picked up her cane. "I've got it. You stay out here and entertain your friend. I'll be back out in a few minutes."

His grandmother went inside. Jasmine got up and sat next to him on the porch step. "Your family is amazing. Did you know you were one of the founding families?"

He laughed. "I'd heard a rumor once."

She shook her head. "Sorry, of course you knew. It's just so interesting. There's so much history in this small town. History that would have been lost if you hadn't helped keep the town going. You're such a good guy."

He leaned in and traced a finger down her cheek. "Remember that later when I drop you off at your place."

"Don't get too cocky," she said. She reached over and toyed with a button on his shirt. "You stood me up last night."

Kevin groaned. "Not on purpose. I was helping a friend." And if he would have known it would take so long to talk with the police, he would have waited to give his statement today and spent the night in Jasmine's arms.

"Fine, I'll give you a pass for last night." She leaned in close. "There is still room for me to change my mind."

"I get that. But are you ready to admit that there is something between us?" That there was something simmering beneath the lust they both felt that deserved exploration.

She held up the camera that was still on the strap around her neck. "There is something between us."

Kevin pulled the camera off her and set it next to him. He took her cheek in his hand and leaned close. "Nothing between us now."

"Are you sure that's not a bad thing?"

If it were, he didn't want to explore that. His retirement, inability to make a relationship work, the failure of his body. None of that would matter if they were together for a summer. One last summer before his life went to hell. "Oh no, ma'am. This is definitely a good thing."

He kissed her. She sighed and leaned in closer. They could be interrupted, he needed to get her home before his kids arrived, but he really wanted to touch her. Feel the warm weight of her breast in his hand. As if that was an order instead of a stray thought, his hand went to the hem of her shirt and slipped beneath. Her skin was smooth and warm against his fingertips. He wanted to kiss every inch of her.

Forgetting where he was, his hand traveled up her side. She trembled. Her mouth opened, granting him access to the sweet depths. The taste of her made him want to lay her back on the porch and strip her naked right then.

He lifted his hand to boldly cup one firm breast. Her answering moan made his dick rock hard. He gently squeezed her breast. Her nipple was plump against his palm, but something hard and firm caressed his hand, too. He pulled back and stared into her eyes.

"Did I just find another piercing?"

Her answering smile made his testosterone levels fly to the moon. "One of two."

He ran his thumb over the small bar. Pictured it in his mind. Her pert, dark nipple pierced with a slim metal piece of jewelry. How would it feel against his tongue?

How would she react when he ran his tongue over the ornamentation? "Damn, you're driving me crazy."

He wanted to see them. Right. Now.

The sound of high-pitched voices came from inside the house. Voices he recognized. No! They weren't supposed to be here for another few hours. His hand jerked from beneath her shirt and he turned toward the back door with a mixture of frustration and surprise.

"What?" Jasmine asked.

"That sounds like the twins."

The back door flew open and his twin daughter and son ran out screaming, "Daddy!"

Brushing his frustration aside, Kevin jumped up to hug his kids. "What are you two doing here already? I wasn't expecting you until eight."

"Mommy had to go to LA for a photo shoot," his son, Deshawn, said. "Grandma switched our flight."

His daughter Mya tugged on the leg of his pants. "Aren't you glad to see us, Daddy?"

He gently pulled on one of her curly pigtails. "Of course I am." Both of his kids had the golden tan coloring of their Filipino mother, but instead of Hanna's straight, dark hair, their precious heads were adorned with curly sandy locks.

"Who's that?" Deshawn pointed to Jasmine.

Jasmine stood. She rubbed her hands on her pants and smiled. Her smile was tight. Uncomfortable. "I'm Jasmine. I'm taking pictures of your dad's property for a project." She said the words as if she were explaining to the principal why she was hanging out in the hall instead of being in class. She threw him a nervous look.

An unsettling thought crept through his mind. Did she not like kids?

Mya's face lit up. "Pictures? Can I see?"

"Maybe later," Kevin said.

"Yes, later," Jasmine said quickly. She looked at her watch. "I'm running late. I've really got to go."

"Stay for a little while. I'll take you home soon."

His grandmother came out. "Yes, dinner is ready and Kevin's mom is home. You should stay and eat."

Jasmine shook her head. "Oh no, I don't want to intrude."

"Girl, hush, you've got to eat."

Kevin agreed. Her last snack was an hour ago and he wasn't ready for her to leave. If she didn't like kids, then that was an automatic no deal for him. He had four. He couldn't be with a woman who had a problem with that, but Jasmine didn't come across as the type of woman who would dislike kids. Disappointment settled around him.

"I've really got to get back to my room. I'm feeling a little tired." She hurried over to his grandmother and gave her a quick hug. "Thank you so much for telling me your family's story." She pulled away and glanced at the kids. "It was nice meeting you." She looked at Kevin. Fear glossed her eyes. "Umm…call me later, okay?" She turned and damn near ran off the porch.

"What was that about?" Charlotte asked.

Kevin watched Jasmine's retreating figure. Fear? Another unsettling thought hit him. Was she feeling bad again? Did she want to get out of there because she was sick? Worry crept up his spine.

He turned to his grandmother. "I don't know," he said. "But I'll find out."

Chapter 11

Back in her room, showered and dressed for bed, the second thoughts crept into Jasmine's mind. She shouldn't have run away from Kevin like that. More important, she shouldn't have panicked the way she had. As soon as she'd seen the kids, she'd panicked.

Jada would say the emotional post-traumatic stress had kicked in.

Maybe that's what happened. One second, her feelings for Kevin had swelled. He'd said there was something between them and she'd forgotten all about this thing being a one-and-done situation. The next second, his kids ran in and all of the reasons why she shouldn't get attached again slapped her in the face.

Julio had given her a glimpse of what a long-term relationship could be. She wanted someone there for her in the middle of the night. Someone to ask if she was okay. Someone who wouldn't be angry or resentful because of her decision to not have kids. She'd fallen in love with his kids. Fallen in love with the idea of having a family. Julio had been the promise of things she hadn't considered a part of her life. Imperfect but he'd been there.

Now here she was falling for Kevin. A guy with an ex-wife he was clearly still fond of, an ex-girlfriend he was connected to by twins, and a belief in commitment that was as stable as a burnt-out building. She'd seen heartbreak in her future like a lingering iceberg and had steered her ship out of there.

A knock on the door startled her out of her concerns. She jumped off the bed and went to the door. Looking in the peephole, her pulse sprinted. Kevin!

He looked up and down the hall. His height and sex appeal overwhelmed her through the closed door. She ran sweaty palms over her boy shorts and white tank top. No bra or underwear. This was not the outfit for a confrontation, but she didn't have time to change.

She opened the door. "Hey, what are you doing here?"

He'd changed into track pants and a sleeveless green Jacksonville Gators shirt. Every tattoo-adorned muscle of his arms was a sinful invitation to touch. Kiss. Explore. His dark eyes examined her with the focused intent of an investigative reporter. His gaze paused quickly on her unrestrained breasts. Her nipples hardened.

"I came to check on you. Why did you run out of there so quickly? Are you okay?"

The concern in his voice made her feel even sillier for running. She was having an emotional meltdown and he was worried that something might seriously be wrong.

"I'm fine. Really, I am. I didn't want to get in the way when your kids arrived."

He leaned one shoulder against the doorjamb. "The kids would've been fine."

"Yeah, well, I thought it best that I leave."

"Why?"

"Because…" *A moment of post-traumatic relationship panic* didn't seem like the right answer.

Kevin raised a brow and leaned in closer. "Because why?"

"I didn't want to make things awkward with your kids meeting me." She turned and went into the room.

The door closed. Kevin had followed her into the room. She tried not to think about why she'd invited him in the night before. Tried and failed. Her body wanted him and the thought of him in her room, with the bed just over there, was making her brain want to forget the reasons she should be thinking this through.

"Awkward how? This wasn't a formal introduction. They arrived early."

She didn't walk to the bed. Instead she moved to the desk in the far corner before facing him. "And you weren't concerned about them meeting me?"

"No," he said firmly. "You're doing an important project that benefits the town. That project includes information about my family. You're a friend."

"Do you kiss all of your friends on your grandmother's back porch?" As soon as the hastily spoken words were out of her mouth, she wished she could snatch them back and stuff them away like an unwanted Christmas sweater.

Kevin's body tensed. He'd been crossing the room to come closer, but his feet suddenly stuck to the floor midstep. "Am I missing something? Do you have a problem with meeting my kids?"

"If we weren't *involved*, then I'd say no, but we kinda are, and we're far from the point of introducing kids."

"I wasn't trying to rush into something more serious here." He said the words carefully. "I don't get what the problem is. Do you not like kids?"

She sighed and rubbed her temples. "It's not that I don't like kids. Kids are fine."

"So why did you run?"

"Because seeing your kids made this thing between us feel a lot more serious than I expected. I've been there. Gotten too connected. It hurts when things don't work out. Especially for me." She leaned back until she rested against the desk.

Kevin came over and stood before her. She was barefoot, and he towered over her. She gripped the edge of the desk instead of reaching out to touch him. Feel the strength of his body. Lean into that strength and let it support her.

"What do you mean?"

She met his gaze. "I love kids, but with my health… kids are possible, but the complications and risks are serious. I've made the decision to not take the risks. I lost my mom, and then later I lost my stepmom. I can't put a child through the possibility."

She'd said as much several times before. To her dad, sister and friends. She'd made peace with her decision until she'd fallen in love with Julio's kids. Then the yearning combined with her biological clock to torment her. She couldn't afford to go through that again.

"I still don't understand."

"Kevin, I like you. I'm cool with us exploring what's between us, but I can't put myself out there. I can't get attached to you or your kids, knowing we're temporary. I've done that. It hurts too much. I'll never have my own children, so falling in love with someone else's kids when I know things aren't going to last... I'm not trying to jump into that."

Not with a guy who didn't want her to be a permanent fixture in his life. Not with a guy she could easily fall in love with if she wasn't careful. The boundaries of their relationship had to be clear.

He took a tentative step backward. "Jasmine, I'm not good at relationships. In fact, I've fucked up every one I've been in."

"Yet you get along with both of your exes." He really got along with his ex-wife.

"That's because I refuse to fail as a dad." He tapped his chest. "I love my kids. I'll do anything for them. Making our family work, despite my relationship with my kids' mothers, was nonnegotiable. It took a long time for us to get to the point where everyone gets along, and keeping things that way is all I care about in this world."

His face and voice had lost the cocky sex appeal that usually accompanied his tone. Honesty and conviction strengthened his words. "My kids are the most important thing to me. I wouldn't introduce you to them if I thought for a second knowing you would hurt them. Am I wrong for thinking that?"

She shook her head. "No. I'd never hurt your kids."

Kevin came forward and cupped her face in his hands. "Then don't overthink things. Meeting the kids tonight wasn't that big of a deal. I know how big a step that is."

Of course he did. She was the one having the freak-out moment because she was the one getting attached. "I just want us to be on the same page," she said, trying to sound confident and sure.

She needed to know how he felt. Was he feeling as strongly about their relationship as she, or was he still viewing this as a fling? Her heart was balanced on the edge. One direction all in, the other accepting this as just fun.

His thumbs brushed her cheeks. "Jasmine, let's just enjoy each other and see what happens. I don't like putting names or expectations on things. We're both attracted to each other. We both like each other. We're consenting adults. That's all that matters. We'll keep our situation just be between us. No family. No friends. No explanations to anyone else about what we're doing. How does that sound?"

His offer was exactly like what she needed to hear. Just the two of them doing what they wanted without any expectations. What she said she wanted. Which was good. Right? She could focus on her project and not obsess about what was, or wasn't, going on with her and Kevin.

She took the feelings that sprouted over the past week with him and buried them deep. This was just a fling. Nothing more.

Jasmine wrapped her arms around his neck. She forced their conversation to the back of her mind. Kevin was here in her room. In her arms. She was tired of waiting.

"That sounds perfect."

His sexy mouth covered hers. The kiss started slow

and deliberate, but within seconds, his efforts became hotter, rawer. Thoughts of why, their past, the meaning of everything slipped away with each demanding stroke of his tongue. He kissed her thoroughly and erased everything except for the need to get closer. To get him naked.

With an impatient tug, he pulled on the edge of her tank top. Jasmine lifted her arms above her head. The cool air in the room caressed her naked torso a second later. Kevin's pupils dilated, the hungry look in his brown eyes searing her skin. Her thighs clenched as desire shot like an arrow to her core.

He slowly cupped her bare breasts in his hands. Ran the tips of his fingers over her pierced nipples with gentle strokes. "When did you do this?"

Jasmine gasped and clutched his waist. The small metal bars increased her sensitivity. Every light caress of his finger sent an answering shiver through her. Heightened her awareness of his large hands covering her breasts. Heat pooled, slick and wet, between her legs.

"When I was nineteen and thought it was cool." The actual piercing had hurt like hell, but the increased pleasure that came after they'd healed was more than enough reason for her to keep them.

"They look so damn sexy." His voice trembled with the force of his desire.

Jasmine clenched her inner muscles. "They taste better than they look."

"That's all I needed to hear." Kevin lifted her by the waist in an efficient swoop. She wrapped her legs around his waist. The rigid tip of his tongue darted out and lightly flicked her nipple. Pleasure crashed over her. Her entire body shuddered. He did it again, this time slowly and deliberately. Getting around every single centimeter of the tip.

Her hands gripped the back of his head. Her legs squeezed him and she undulated her hips to try to ease the pressure building between her thighs.

"You like that." It wasn't a question. Instead his voice held a delighted and smug recognition of how his actions sent her body into a tailspin.

"Harder," she whispered.

His lips closed over her nipple and the piercing. He sucked slightly. The decadent feeling spread lava through her veins. Jasmine's head fell back.

Her eyes were squeezed closed tightly, but she felt the movement as he crossed the room. The cool sheets touched her back. Kevin's warm, strong body covered her front.

"No," she panted. "Me on top."

She nudged him with her knees and he rolled over. Jasmine didn't waste time pulling his shirt off. She shimmied down his long body until her feet were on the floor. There she lost her shorts and jerked his off. He'd also gone commando, his erection long and curved. Hell yeah, she loved a curve!

Climbing back up his fantastic body, she relished in the feel of his skin against hers. The heat and tension of his muscles felt as great as she'd imagined from the day she'd photographed him.

Except no fantasy could've prepared her for how addicted she was to the feel of Kevin. She kissed his neck and chest. Her fingers played over the elaborate tattoos. The urge to ask about them fought with her urgency to get him as deep inside of her as she could. While she kissed and explored, his hands did their own expedition over her back, sides and breasts.

The controlled strength of his hands as he gripped her hips and thighs only excited her more. She knew he was powerful. Had seen the play of muscles as she'd photographed him. Saw his dominance on the basketball court. But the gentle, almost reverent touch of his hands on her body only made her want to watch him lose control.

She sat up and reached under her pillow for the condom she'd placed there the night before.

"You were ready," he said with a cocky grin that made her sex weep.

"It's from last night," she said, matching his smile. "But I've been ready from the second I looked at you."

His eyes widened. Oh crap. She hadn't meant to say that. His hands slid up her thighs until his thumbs brushed the secret spot between her legs. With gentle but firm circular motions, he teased the sensitive nub peeking out for his attention. "So have I." His lids drooped as he continued to caress her. "You feel so damn good."

"Wait until you're inside me." Her voice was a throaty whisper she almost didn't recognize. With ease, she opened the condom and slid the protection over his length.

Kevin's eyes didn't leave hers as she took him in her hand, lifted her body, then eased down on him. "Oh damn," she hissed between her teeth. He stretched and filled her until she thought he would touch every part of her. "You're so…"

His grin widened. "I know." His fingers dug into her

waist. Tighter and tighter until the length of his cock completely impaled her.

She didn't give a damn if she'd inflated his already gigantic ego. Kevin was more than enough for her and she was ready for the ride. She rocked her hips and they got into a groove. His upward thrusts met her downward plunge. He watched her through slitted lids, his mouth falling open as she took both of them to new heights.

She couldn't look away—the pleasure on his face mesmerizing her, the working of his Adam's apple as he swallowed. The labored rise and fall of his chest. How his eyes rolled back when she took him completely.

She couldn't keep this up for long. He felt too good. Was so deep. Exquisite pleasure expanded inside her like a hot air balloon. She was about to explode.

His hands cupped her breasts. Fingers pinched her sensitive nipples. Her body detonated on a wave of pleasure, her head falling back, her spine arching as she cried out. He tensed, then jerked beneath her. Following her over the edge.

Panting and sweating, Jasmine fell forward onto his chest. The heavy sound of his breathing and the pounding of his heart lulled her into a trance. She wasn't sure how long they stayed like that. She could have stayed there forever. She didn't want to examine that too much. Great sex tended to cloud judgment.

Kevin's hand ran up and down her back. He chuckled. Jasmine was too spent to lift her head and look at him. "That better be a good laugh," she mumbled.

"That was an *I think I've found my weakness and I*

don't even care laugh," he said. His voice was deep and husky from his own groans.

She smiled, satisfied and glowing with her own smugness as she listened to the steady beat of his heart.

Chapter 12

Kevin shifted where he sat on the bed of his grandmother's truck and pulled his cell phone out of his back pocket. Jasmine was taking pictures of Rachel's great-great-grandparents' home. She'd traded in her high-heeled boots for a pair of sneakers and her long legs were out for his appraisal thanks to the denim shorts she wore. Excitement made her dark eyes spark with life as she darted around the property, snapping pictures.

He navigated to his phone's camera and got his own shots of her. The trees filtered the sunlight and combined with the breeze to make the hot early afternoon moderately comfortable. The house was still in relatively good shape. Rachel's uncle still farmed the land around it, so her family hadn't let the old home go into disrepair.

He had to admit he'd learned a little more about his town in the past two weeks with Jasmine. He had a decent history of the families there because most people talked about how the mill owners had stolen their legacy. But hearing more stories firsthand as he'd gone around with Jasmine had made him appreciate being part of one of the founding families.

He was glad he'd invested here, and supported Jasmine's project even more to ensure the rest of the families in Silver Springs got the recognition they deserved.

He was due to leave town tomorrow. He had a meeting with his agent, then the team leaders. Everyone wanted him to re-sign. He wanted to resign. The pain in his fingers, wrist and knees made the decision for him. After his announcement, everything would change. He'd be a has-been.

"Why are you frowning?" Jasmine's voice broke his thoughts.

She walked back over to him. She'd knotted the front of her T-shirt and he caught a glimpse of her pink belly button ring. She had nine piercings: six in her ears, one belly ring, plus the two he loved the most. She also had three tattoos—an outline of a camera at the small of her back, the words Capture Life around her ankle and the small heart on the front of her shoulder. He'd succeeded in discovering all her hidden treasures, yet he still wanted more.

"I leave tomorrow. Thinking about the meetings ahead."

He thought he saw sadness in her gaze but a bird chirped in the trees above and Jasmine looked up. "When is your first meeting?"

She didn't sound upset about him leaving. They'd made no promises. She'd insisted on making it clear their relationship was just for fun. Which was what he was good at, but he wanted to keep seeing her. Wanted more of her, even though he knew she too would see him as past his prime once he announced his retirement.

"Day after tomorrow. I'm going to Jacksonville to help with the summer camp the team does every year. While I'm there, I'll meet with the team owners and discuss my future as a Gator."

She looked back at him. "So you're staying on the team?"

He flexed his fingers. The pain wasn't bad today. He'd succumbed to taking the medication every day. "I don't think so." He didn't want to stop playing, but he also didn't want to jeopardize his health any further.

Jasmine's soft fingers closed in over his hand. "You okay?" Her eyes were concerned. Her touch comforting.

For a second, he considered telling her. About the rheumatoid arthritis diagnosis. The fear of his body breaking down. The end of the only career he'd known. But that was stressful and upsetting. They'd only agreed to fun.

"I'm good. Just getting ready for a change." He shifted and spread his legs so she could stand between them. "I've played ball professionally since I was eighteen. It's a little weird to think of doing something else." He took her camera out of her hands and lifted the strap from around her neck.

The camera strap mussed her hair and she combed the blue-tipped strands back down with her fingers. "Any new ideas of what you'll be doing?"

"I've been thinking about real estate." The dappled sunlight played across her shoulders and chest. He traced a trail to each place the sun touched her brown skin. Her breathing hitched, and pleasure swelled in his chest. She hadn't tired of him either, and that only added to his determination to keep her in his bed.

"Real estate? Why real estate?" She rubbed her hands along his thighs. A major part of his anatomy noticed the proximity of her touch.

"Because of what I was able to do here in Silver Springs. A few smart investments helped save the town. Maybe I can keep doing that. Take places people think are old and obsolete and show that they're still viable. Once the mill left, other businesses began to write off our town. But I knew the potential—I'd always seen what Silver Springs could be. There have to be other places like this that just need a little boost."

"Have you invested in real estate elsewhere?" Her hand creeped farther up his thigh.

"A few other locations. Most of my business investments have been in new products related to sports, but I have invested in a few start-up companies. I haven't had a bad investment yet. So far, I've been able to increase my net worth without only relying on playing and endorsements."

He tried to sound excited about his future. Sure, he'd made money and had no problems with making more. But investing had been a fun side hustle. His love was basketball. No amount of money would make up for the hole left when he wasn't a part of the league anymore.

Her hands stopped. Her eyes lit up with surprise. "I remember you saying you've invested. Obviously, you're good at choosing what to support."

He shrugged. "I've just been lucky. I go with my instincts and I listen to the pitch. When the idea doesn't feel right, I don't invest. I skipped college to play professionally. After my divorce, I went back and got a business degree. Learned a few things."

"Smart and sexy." She leaned in and pressed her full lips against his. "That's really damn hot."

He slid his hand beneath her shirt. Caressed her silky-smooth skin. Her body was long and lush. Plenty of curves to cushion a man and make him want to hold her close all night long. If anyone was sexy, it was her. "If you think that's sexy, I'll be happy to show you my degree. How hot will that make me?"

Her arms wrapped around his neck. "There isn't much you could do to be hotter."

"Oh really?" He lifted her by the waist onto the truck bed next to him. The sudden movement made her shriek, then laugh.

"What are you doing?"

He'd spread out a blanket in the truck bed while she took pictures. He gently pushed her backward and covered her body with his. "Kissing you."

He covered her mouth with his. She opened and welcomed him without hesitation. Her kisses were addictive. One was never enough, and after one touch of her lips, he couldn't stop himself from kissing her again and again. Getting her out of his system seemed impossible, but he didn't want to lose the high she put him on.

He didn't want to think about his future. Didn't want to think about the disappointment of walking away from the only career he'd known. When he was with Jasmine, he didn't think of that and that was what he wanted at this moment. To forget everything but the bliss he found in her arms.

She twisted and moved beneath him as if trying to get closer. Her hands pushed under his shirt. The slight hurt of her nails as she gripped along his back made his heart punch against his rib cage. She pulled on his shirt. He didn't hesitate to rise up and toss it over his head. Her eyes were warm and dark with growing desire.

"You ever had sex in the back of a truck?" he asked.

Jasmine pulled off her tank top and unhooked her bra. "I'm about to."

The husky confidence in her voice sent a surge to his dick. Kevin kissed her with all the need coursing through him. He jerked off her pants. His movements were uncoordinated tugs made clumsy by his anxiousness, and, dammit, his stiff hands. Then finally, finally, her curves and skin were unhindered against his.

Paradise and luxury. That's what the softness of her body was to him. The lushness of her curves and the scent that was all her. She was a work of art to enjoy. A delicacy to savor, and savor her was what he planned to do.

Taking his time, he kissed every inch of her body, spending extra time with her awesome breasts. He'd seen nipple rings before. Jasmine didn't put hers on display with flimsy see-through tops and no bra. The fact that they were hidden, a delight for him to unwrap, drove him even crazier with want.

By the time he'd slipped on the condom and positioned himself at her entrance, her hands clawed at his arms and shoulders. The whimpers and noises she made… God, he could listen to her every day. Could do whatever he needed to get her to make them and delight in knowing she was as into this as he was.

He slid in deep and something in his chest sang.

"Mmm, Kevin, yes," Jasmine moaned. Her nails dug into his back.

He wanted to see her. Bracing himself on one arm, he watched her face as they made love. Captivated by the absolute, uninhibited pleasure that crossed her features. He took his time. Focused, taking in every nuance of this moment, how beautiful she looked, how good she felt! Anything to prolong this moment. When her back arched and her body clenched around his, he finally let go and succumbed to the pleasure.

He lay over her, still keeping most of his weight off her. A breeze blew over them. He shivered as the air rushed over his sweat-slickened back. Unable to stop himself, he kissed her forehead, cheek and lips.

"Meet me in Jacksonville week after next," he said against her lips.

Her body stiffened. He raised his head and met her eyes. They were full of questions. "You want to keep seeing me after you leave?"

"Yes."

"Why?"

"Because the idea of this being the last time I see you is something I can't accept." He kissed her soft lips. Slid over to her ear. "Can you?"

His tongue darted out and tasted the sweat of their lovemaking still on her skin. His hips shifted, pushing deeper, because he hadn't been able to make himself draw away.

Her soft gasp caressed his cheek. "I can't."

"Then say you'll see me again."

"I thought you just wanted fun."

"I just want you." He did. He wasn't ready for a relationship. Wasn't ready to face failing at another relationship. But he wasn't ready to say goodbye to Jasmine either. They didn't have to put a name on what they were doing. As long as they both wanted to keep seeing each other, then that was all that mattered.

The smile that brightened her face vacuum-sealed his resolve to make her smile every day he was with her.

"Then I'll come see you in Jacksonville."

Chapter 13

"You've got to be kidding me. You've got at least two more good seasons in you."

Kevin looked up from the cup of coffee he wasn't drinking into the incredulous eyes of his agent, Clive Green. Kevin started working with Clive ten years ago, after realizing his first agent, who'd snatched Kevin up the second he showed potential in high school, didn't have his best interests at heart. Clive had done wonders for his career. Gotten him better endorsement deals and sparked his interest in using his money in other areas to help spread his wealth.

"This isn't a joke," Kevin said. He looked around the restaurant, but no one had overheard. He and Clive met here often when they needed to discuss business. Many Gators players attended the place and the owner always put them at tables near the back where they could discuss business without being in the direct line of sight of the other patrons.

"I've thought things over and my mind is made up. I'm not going to renew my contract with the Gators," Kevin told him.

Clive shifted in his seat and drew his brows together. "Do you mind telling me why? You're at a good place with the Gators. Your championship run has made you the hottest team out there and you are a major reason why they've done well. The owners are ready to offer you a lot of money to renew with them."

Kevin tamped back the need to immediately agree. He wanted to play. He was going to miss the team, the guys who'd become friends, the rush of going out onto the court before a game, the joy of winning and even the crush of defeat.

"I don't want to retire," Kevin began. He held up a hand when Clive's eyes lit up. "But I can't play anymore. The aches and pains in my hands and knees aren't just soreness. I've got rheumatoid arthritis. What I want doesn't matter. My body is telling me to stop."

Clive shook his head. He tugged on the neck of his white button-up shirt as if it were choking him. "That's ridiculous. You're young."

"I know. It's not the typical diagnosis for someone my age. That's why my doctor didn't test me for years. But he did after I dropped the ball in the playoffs. I knew then that something was off."

"This doesn't mean you have to quit playing. There has to be a way around this. Drugs, exercises, something you can do?" Clive ticked off each idea on his fingers.

As if Kevin hadn't gone through each of these scenarios. "We're working on a treatment, but that doesn't mean I can keep playing. I need to take care of myself.

I've played ball since I was eighteen. It's time for me to consider other things."

He tried to infuse his voice with confidence. If Clive got a hint of Kevin's inner turmoil and bitterness over the breakdown of his body, then he'd try to talk Kevin into staying. Kevin hated leaving, but he didn't want to make his body break down faster because of his pride. He'd find a way to spend the next thirty to forty years of his life. He swallowed coffee to stop the scowl.

Clive tilted his head to the side. "Arthritis? Really?"

The coffee was bitter and cold. Kevin pushed his cup to the side and leaned back in his chair. "I wish it was a joke."

"Have you told anyone else?"

"No. I wanted to tell you before I broke the news to the team."

"I appreciate that." Clive sat forward and met Kevin's eyes, his expression the one of determination he got when talking to Kevin about his career. "Look, I don't like that you're quitting, but I guess I understand. We'll manage your exit. Play up the fact that you're stepping back for your health. Get the team to pay tribute to you. They owe you for your work on the team. I may even be able to work out some new endorsements for you. Drug companies are always looking for celebrities for endorsements. We can also find ways to keep you in the game. I heard *Sports Reporter* is looking for another host for their basketball show."

Kevin slowly sat up. "Wait a minute, you still want to represent me?"

"Why wouldn't I?" Clive sounded almost offended.

"Because my basketball career is over. I thought you'd want to move on."

"Kevin, when I signed on with you, it wasn't just to work with you until you quit playing ball. Many players go on to have successful careers after they leave. You can, too. The arthritis thing is a hitch in your plans, but it doesn't mean your career is over. Unless you don't want to work with me anymore."

"No—I do." A weight lifted off his shoulders. He'd assumed once he announced he was leaving that everything in his life related to basketball would fade away. The team wouldn't care anymore, his agent, his teammates. Sure, everyone was cool, but at the end of the day, the sport was also a business. When he'd planned to start over, he had thought he would have to start all the way over. Clive's willingness to stick by his side gave Kevin hope that others in this part of his life would, too.

"I couldn't imagine working with anyone else." Kevin held out his hand.

Clive shook it and smiled. "Good. Now let's get our game plan together before we meet with the team. If you've got to leave the league, at least you're going to leave in style."

"Are you coming home soon?"

Jasmine rolled her eyes before narrowing them at her cell phone lying on the bed next to her suitcase. Her sister's whine had lost its ability to sway her decisions years ago. That didn't stop Jada from trying.

"Why are you suddenly in a rush for me to come home?" Jasmine asked. "You know I'm not planning on heading back until the end of the summer."

"Where are you going? You just said you were packing. You can come here."

Jasmine folded another shirt and slipped it into her bag. "What's going on, Jada? Is something wrong with Dad?"

"No."

"Is something wrong with you?"

"No." Her sister's reply was petulant.

"Okay, then, there's no reason for me to come home ahead of schedule."

Jada's heavy sigh echoed in Jasmine's hotel room. "Kathy is coming to town next week," Jada said in a rush. "Remember I said she wants to see us."

Jasmine shook her head and pointed at the phone. "Oh no. Remember I said I didn't want to see her?"

"Jasmine, don't be like that. She's our mom."

Jasmine snatched up her cell phone and brought the speaker closer to her face. "No. She is not our mom. She was our stepmom."

"She raised us, Jasmine. In my book, that makes her our mom."

Jasmine closed her eyes and pinched the bridge of her nose. Jada didn't remember their mom. Kathy was her only memory of a maternal figure. She'd been just as hurt as Jasmine when Kathy divorced their dad and moved away.

But instead of being smart and channeling her hurt into anger, like Jasmine had done, Jada had turned her hurt into an obsession with knowing what Kathy was up to. Jada was the reason Jasmine knew as much as she did about her former stepmother. Jada cyber-stalked Kathy on social media and insisted on sending Christmas and birthday cards in an effort to let Kathy know they still cared. Kathy had never returned the gesture.

"Our mom died. Kathy stepped in for a while, then she moved on. We don't owe her anything. Obviously, she didn't feel as if she owed us anything when she left without keeping in touch."

"She wants to see us. Can you please come home and see her?"

"No."

"Fine, but I'm going to meet with her and I don't want you to give me any crap about it."

Jasmine rolled her eyes and held up a hand. She looked skyward and prayed for patience. "If you want to waste your time listening to her justify why she didn't bother to talk to us for years, go ahead," she said slowly.

"She and Dad divorced. She was hurt. I don't see you calling up Julio and talking to his kids." Jada's high, sharp words pierced Jasmine's pride.

Jasmine sucked in a breath. "Because Julio is back with his wife. His kids have a mother."

"But if Julio wasn't with her, you can't tell me you wouldn't want to talk to his kids. That you wouldn't be curious about what they're up to. I know you loved his kids. Maybe Kathy feels the same. How can you not understand why she wouldn't want to reconnect with us?"

"My situation is different," she snapped, but Jada's argument struck a chord.

Jasmine had loved Julio's kids. Not being around them anymore had been another hard part of the breakup. She'd had no place in their life after he went back to his ex-wife. How would that look? The rebound girlfriend still coming around while he and his wife reconciled. Talk about uncomfortable family dinners.

So, yes, she could get why Kathy would step back, but her dad hadn't had anyone else. There was no mother or ex-wife that Kathy would have had to deal with. Kathy had been their mother for nearly ten years and she'd walked away from them without a backward glance to replace them with another, better family.

"Fine, be stubborn," Jada said, exasperated. "But you want to talk to her as much as I do. You just want to be stubborn."

Stubborn or not, Jasmine wasn't putting herself in another situation that would only disappoint and hurt her. If Jada wanted to do this, fine. Jasmine only hoped her sister didn't get hurt in the process.

"Just promise me you won't get your hopes up if you meet her. Don't expect things to be all honey and lemonade. You may not like what you hear."

"I won't." Jada let out a breath. A few seconds later, when her sister spoke, her voice was more upbeat. "Now, are you going to tell me where you're going? You've only been in Greenville for a week and you were in that Silver Springs place for two."

She'd spent the past week with Mr. Tatum, photographing a home that had belonged to the county's first black doctor. The family had moved away but still owned the place. Jasmine had plans to call the doctor's great-grandson to find out more about the family.

"I've got to make a quick weekend trip. I'll be back in the area next week."

"Uh-huh…you're going to see him again." Her sister's reply was smug.

"You don't have to say it like that."

"Yes, I do," Jada said in a singsong voice. "Are you two dating now?"

"Kevin and I are just having fun. There's no need to define what we're doing."

Except that in the two weeks since he'd left to go back to Jacksonville, they'd talked on the phone nearly every day, texted constantly and sexted almost as much. He'd surprised her by meeting her in Greenville when she'd gotten there last Friday. They'd spent most of the weekend in bed. A smile crept on her lips.

"But you're talking a lot and taking weekends together. Are you sure you're not together?"

"Look, it was one weekend, not weekends."

"Nah, sorry, sister. This weekend makes it plural."

Jasmine cursed to herself. "We're not dating. Not really."

They talked about her project. He mentioned meetings with the team and making plans for retirement, but not what those plans were or why he was retiring when he clearly didn't want to. He didn't bring up his kids. She didn't talk about her family. They were doing what they said they would do.

"You need to figure that out," Jada said as if she'd just read her sister's mind. "What if he's out there sleeping around with a bunch of other people?"

"We're together enough, okay. I mean, there aren't any reports of him being seen with anyone else. He doesn't freak out about the needles, and even makes sure I'm feeling okay. Just because we haven't said anything doesn't mean he's sleeping around. We're having fun."

"Spoken like a delusional woman," Jada said. "Don't settle for years of undefined fun if that's not what you want."

"Who says this isn't what I want?" She liked what she had going with Kevin. Questioning him about the actual terms of their relationship would make her seem as if she was trying to rush into something. She wasn't.

Really. She wanted a relationship one day. For now, why couldn't she just enjoy what they had going?

"What happens when the fun run ends?" Jada asked seriously. "You should end things with him now. Before you're too caught up in this *undefined* situation you've got going with him."

"I'm fine. We aren't talking marriage or anything. I won't get hurt."

"But you want marriage and all that. You told me so after Julio. Don't go down the same path."

Damn tequila shots and a broken heart. Inner secrets were supposed to stay that way. Not blurted out in a moment of alcohol-supported weakness for sisters to toss back at inappropriate times.

"I'm not." Jasmine's voice was tight. "Look, I've got to finish packing. I'll give you a call later."

Jada sighed. "Fine. Do you. Have fun with the player."

"And you do you. Meet with the woman who abandoned us."

"You know what. I'll talk to you later."

"Yeah, later." Jasmine ended the call and tossed the phone back on the bed.

Her gaze strayed over to the bag of new lingerie she'd purchased the day before. Something sexy for her meeting with Kevin. Just the idea of him peeling the black lace off her had gotten her slick and ready in the store.

Maybe she was a little addicted to the great sex. Walking away from good sex was about as hard as nailing a perfect score on the SATs.

Besides, the good sex hadn't clouded her judgment. They talked, had great conversations, seemed to vibe, but weren't lovers supposed to? She knew what was

up. They'd made that clear. She wasn't falling in love.
She was not in danger of putting Kevin in a position to
break her heart.

Jada was crazy and obviously not thinking straight.
She was meeting Kathy, for goodness' sake. Not the
person to take advice from.

Jasmine's phone chimed. She tossed the lingerie in
the overnight bag and swiped up her phone. A text from
Kevin was on screen.

I can't wait to see you tomorrow. I miss you.

Jasmine bit her lip and grinned. Her heart raced with
excitement. This was what having fun was all about.
There was no harm in having fun.

She pulled out the lingerie, arranged the sexy black
lace on the bed and snapped a photo. Quickly she sent
the picture with a kiss emoji and her response:

Missing you, too.

Chapter 14

Kevin wasn't sure what was the best way to announce to his teammates that he was leaving. He just knew doing it via press conference or company memo wasn't the route to take. Beers and barbecue seemed much better.

He pulled two beers from the outdoor fridge next to his grill. His teammate Jacobe teased Kevin about his elaborate backyard cooking setup that included a charcoal and gas grill, wood smoker and a fish cleaning station. Mostly because, for all of his gadgets, Kevin only used the items once or twice a year. When he did, it was typically for a big get-together at his house. Today's invitation had only gone out to the three other guys he considered friends on the team: Isaiah, Will and Jacobe. They deserved to hear the news first.

He popped the top on one beer and passed the second to Isaiah. His three friends lounged in the extra-large sofas and chairs on his stone patio. The smell of hickory wood chips in the smoker filled the air.

Isaiah took the beer from Kevin and opened it. His clean-cut best friend looked ready for a debate club meeting in his perfectly pressed blue polo shirt and khaki shorts. The smile that perpetually graced his face since asking his girlfriend, Angela, to marry him was still there. "Kevin, how much longer until those ribs are ready? I'm about to go directly into your smoker and eat them."

Kevin laughed and glanced at the black smokehouse. "I put them in at five this morning. They'll be ready soon. I want to tell you guys something first."

Will rubbed his beard, then pointed at Jacobe. "See, I told you there was something going on." Will, the easygoing member of their group, had spent most of the morning checking the Instagram likes on a picture he posted the night before and sending messages to the latest woman in his string of flings. He put his phone down and focused on Kevin.

Jacobe held out his hand toward Kevin. "Hold up. Let the man talk first." Once considered the wild card of the league, Jacobe had mellowed out completely after getting married the year before. Now the guy most likely to start a fight on the court was not only the poster child for happy married men, he was the biggest champion for the environment in their city, thanks in part to a huge influence from his wife.

"Thank you," Kevin said. "Though Will is right. There is something going on."

Isaiah shifted forward in his seat. "Is everything okay?"

Kevin rubbed his knees—they weren't bothering

him as much today—then looked at the three guys who were the closest he had to brothers. "I'm announcing my retirement in a few weeks."

The level of surprise on their faces wasn't unexpected.

Will shook his head. "Hell, no. You're a key member of this team."

Jacobe put his beer down. "Kevin, you can't be serious. We're on a roll."

Isaiah took a deep breath. His dark eyes looked at Kevin with understanding. "It's the RA. Isn't it?"

Of the three, Isaiah was the one Kevin was closest to. They'd struck up a friendship despite their age difference and opposite personalities. Isaiah was more reserved than Kevin, but his measured personality meant he often served as a sounding board whenever Kevin needed to talk. He'd noticed Kevin's stiffness during the season and told him it was more than sore muscles. He'd been the first person Kevin called after getting the diagnosis.

Jacobe looked from Isaiah to Kevin. "RA? What the hell is RA?"

"Rheumatoid arthritis," Kevin said. "I was diagnosed after the playoffs." He brought his friends up to speed on the conversation he'd had with his agent and their plans to try to find a way to keep him connected to the league in some way.

All three were silent for several seconds after Kevin finished talking. Will met his gaze and nodded. "Kevin, you know we've got you."

"I'm sorry I let you guys down. Let the team down," Kevin said.

Jacobe shook his head. "You aren't letting anyone

down. Are we disappointed to see you go? Yeah, but we understand why. Your health is way more important than the team."

"He's right," Isaiah said. "We're going to miss you on the court, but just because you aren't playing doesn't mean you're not still a part of the team. Take care of yourself, man."

Man law said Kevin should blame the warmth in his chest on the sunlight. He'd been crazy for thinking he'd lose this, his friendship with his boys.

Will stood. "You know what this means?" He walked over to the smoker. "You'll have plenty of time to fire up your toys. I expect major feasts after each Gators win."

Kevin laughed. He got up and strolled over to Will. "Feasts?"

"Hell yeah," Will said. "I'm talking burgers, ribs, Boston butts, brisket and everything. You've got enough here to open your own steak house."

Kevin checked the ribs through the panel. "I'll think about that. For now, these ribs are ready. Let's eat."

Kevin got out the ribs. They ate, talked about the upcoming season, Isaiah's wedding plans and Jacobe's eagerness to start a family. It was a good day that further cemented his friendship with his brothers by choice.

Isaiah stuck around after Will and Jacobe left, and they moved from the back patio to the game room. Kevin's cell phone buzzed. He checked and smiled at the text from Jasmine. She would be there tomorrow morning. Even though he enjoyed his friends' company, if he could snap his finger to make them disappear and have Jasmine there instead, he would do so.

They'd spent a few weekends together and still, that wasn't enough. She was back in Georgia and would be for the next few weeks. He was going to Atlanta the following week to catch up with his oldest daughters. When he was in Atlanta, he spent as much time with his girls as possible.

But with Jasmine so close he wanted to spend time with her, as well. Remembering her last freak-out, he was going to have to do a little maneuvering to manage his time without her crossing paths with his kids. He'd done that before with other women. Doing so with Jasmine didn't feel the same. His daughters would like her. He wanted them to like her.

"When are you going to tell me what's up with you and this woman?" Isaiah asked after Kevin texted back, telling Jasmine he'd meet her at her hotel.

"What do you mean, what's up?" Kevin slipped his phone back in his pocket. He picked up the bottle of water he'd grabbed to counteract the beers from earlier and took a swig.

"Are you two serious?" Isaiah asked.

"Serious? Why would you automatically go there?"

Isaiah raised a brow. "Because you've spent several weekends with her."

"I've spent several weekends with other women," Kevin said.

"Yeah, but none of the women make you smile like this. I recognize that smile. It's the same one I get when I think about Angela."

"Oh, we're analyzing smiles now?" Kevin asked with a raised brow.

"Yeah, so spill it. Who is she and how long has this been going on?"

"Her name is Jasmine," Kevin said, deciding not to

go into the meaning of his smile. "I met her during the *Sports Fitness* shoot. We've been hanging out over the summer."

"Are y'all exclusive?"

They hadn't talked about exclusivity. He hadn't slept with anyone else. Not that he would do that anyway. He'd break things off before moving on. The thing was, he didn't want to move on. He didn't think she was sleeping with anyone else either, but he couldn't really demand that she be exclusive when they weren't putting a name on what they were doing.

"It's complicated," Kevin answered.

Isaiah raised a brow. "Complicated? Either you're getting serious with her or you're not. How is this complicated?"

Not being sure about what he wanted to do with this thing between him and Jasmine complicated things. "Because, defining what we're doing creates expectations. Expectations I'm not ready to deal with. I've done the messy breakup before. I don't want to do that anymore."

Isaiah shook his head. "You're already thinking about messy breakups? Come on, man, you can't be thinking about the end when you're just getting started."

"I disagree. You have to think about the fallout if things don't go right before you get into something," Kevin replied. That's why he preferred keeping things casual. Casual meant a clean break followed by moving on. "I'm trying to keep things chill."

"Kevin, man, I know you don't want to get married again. That doesn't mean you can't go ahead and say this Jasmine woman is more than a casual affair.

So what if she puts expectations on you? You're a decent dude."

"I'm a decent dude with an uncertain future, a body breaking down on me, four kids and two women whose hearts I've already broken. I'm not trying to drag anyone else into that." He wouldn't have admitted as much if Jacobe and Will were still there. He trusted Isaiah a little more to see the frustration that was his failure at making relationships work. A legacy left to him by his father.

"If she knows about all of that, and she's cool with that, then that's for her to decide. Everybody has issues, man. You telling me Jasmine's perfect?"

Perfect for him. "She's got her own stuff."

"Does that make you like her any less?"

"No."

Isaiah shrugged. "Well, then. Don't be afraid to take this casual thing you've got and make it a little more permanent."

"How am I supposed to do that?"

"Angela is planning a couples night tomorrow. Bring Jasmine."

"We said no friends."

Isaiah stood and slipped his car keys from his pocket. "Was that before or after you realized you're feeling more for her than just what's between her legs?"

Jasmine had intrigued him from the start. Keeping this noncommittal was supposed to keep him from ultimately hurting her. What if he failed to give her what she needed just as he had with Sabrina and Hanna? What if he couldn't be there for her? Especially now that he had the RA to deal with?

But what if you can? What if you could do better?

Isaiah lightly punched Kevin's shoulder as he walked to the door. "Tomorrow at eight. You've got a lot of changes in your life right now. This one could be positive."

Kevin considered his friend's words long after he'd left.

Chapter 15

Jasmine watched the lights flash by from the passenger seat of Kevin's large SUV. They were crossing the Buckman Bridge over the Saint Johns River on their way to a party at Kevin's teammate's home. She'd gotten in the night before and had greeted Kevin at her hotel room door wearing nothing but a silky robe. They'd spent the rest of the night and following day in bed.

Later that afternoon, after they'd gone out for food and come back to his place, he'd broached the subject.

"I know we said no friends, but one of my teammates is having a get-together at his house tonight. I thought we might swing through," he'd said while they'd lounged on the couch. They were supposed to be watching a movie but had spent the first thirty minutes kissing like teenagers on a first date.

"Yeah, sure." She'd tried to keep a no-big-deal quality to her voice, though excitement trickled through her veins. She was taking her sister's advice and had decided to figure out what to do about her and Kevin. They'd been sleeping together for over a month, and she knew the time was coming for her to end things before she lost her heart.

The corner of his lips twitched, then a slow sexy smile spread across his handsome face. "You sure?"

She'd been lying on top of him on the couch. Beneath her hands resting on his chest, she could feel the steady, heavy beat of his heart. His dark gaze asked a question she too was afraid to verbalize. Were they ready to take another step forward?

She'd nodded and leaned in to kiss him. "I'm sure."

Now as they were on their way to hang out with his friends, their relationship status was about all she could think about. God, she wasn't supposed to be here. She was supposed to have learned from her mistakes. The smart thing to do would be to break things off now and move on. She didn't want marriage now, but one day she would. Guys like Kevin were fun flings. Not serious long-term hookups.

Kevin's warm hand covered hers where it rested on her knee. "Why are you so quiet?"

She turned away from the passing lights to face him. Even in the dim glow, he took her breath away. He wore a stylish, light gray T-shirt and darker gray slacks, both of which brought out the perfectly toned muscles in his large body. He glanced at her from the corner of his sexy dark eyes.

"Thinking about things."

"Oh really?" His full lips tilted up in a smile that made her blood sizzle and pop. "What kind of things?"

"Mostly how much I've enjoyed myself so far this weekend."

He squeezed her hand. "Enjoyed myself is an understatement. You coming to see me is the perfect ending to my visit here."

A warm and fuzzy feeling blossomed in her chest. Jasmine bit her lip to stop the huge grin from spreading across her face. "And why is that?"

"I was really worried about coming back to Jacksonville, talking to my agent and breaking it to the team owners." The flirtation went out of his face and his brows drew together. "I expected things to go badly."

They hadn't talked much about his meetings with the team. Mostly because they hadn't talked about anything too deep. He'd only mentioned that things had gone well.

She could keep things superficial but found herself not wanting to accept that. "Why did you expect things to go badly?"

He lifted and lowered his shoulders. "I don't know. I just thought ending my basketball career would mean ending my connection to the game completely. My agent surprised me. He wants to keep working with me and has ideas for ways to continue to promote me after we announce my retirement. He wants to find ways to keep me connected to the game."

"Oh really, like what?"

He glanced at her out of the corner of his eye. "Broadcasting maybe. Sports reporting?" His tone was questioning. How could he possibly doubt himself? He loved the game, and transitioning to sports reporting would keep him connected.

"That's actually a really great idea," she said. "You've played since you were eighteen. You know the ins and outs of the game and you have an outgoing personality. It sounds kind of perfect for you."

Tension left his shoulders. His hand on hers tightened and the smile he shot her made her feel as if she'd just made his day. "That's what I thought. It's not set in stone. I've still got to see if someone is interested, but Clive is looking out for me."

"I'm glad you're not losing your agent."

"Me, too. I haven't told all of my teammates yet. I dropped the news to the ones closest to me first. The rest of the team will find out on Monday."

"How did they take things?"

"Really well, actually. They hate to see me leave, but they understood my reasons. Taking care of me is the most important thing."

His fingers flexed over her hand. His eyes didn't leave the road, but his brows drew together.

"Taking care of you? Kevin, what's really going on? I know you've said you want to try something new and that you've played ball all your life, but you never told me why now is the time for you to leave. It's obvious you still want to play. Why are you retiring?"

He brought her hand up to his mouth and kissed the back. The brush of his lips across her skin was soft and fleeting. A sizzle of heat traced up her arm and spread through her body. "It's just time. I'm getting older. I'd rather go out on top than wait until people say I should have left years earlier."

Jasmine knew that wasn't the entire story. Something else was going on with Kevin. Something he didn't want to talk to her about. Another sign they weren't really a couple.

"How did it go in Greenville?" he asked.

She fought the urge to glare at him. He wanted to change the subject, fine. *Don't push for more. Realize when more isn't coming and cut all ties.*

"Even better than I expected," she answered. "I got some good shots of the home of one of the area's first black doctors—a woman, if you can believe it. She was from North Carolina and lived in Georgia but stayed in Greenville for a few years. I can't wait for everyone to see the pictures."

"Your project is really cool. I think it's great, the history you're documenting."

"I hope everyone else thinks the same. I got a call from one of my friends who took a job in Milan for *Vogue* I turned down. She's about to be flying first-class, staying in five-star hotels and going to fabulous parties after the shoot. I'm spending my summer—"

"Doing something great that will bring recognition to families who struggled to find an existence during a difficult time," Kevin said with determination. "You want to go to Milan, fine. I'll take you after your show to celebrate. We'll party and stay at the best hotels, but don't think for a second that what you're doing isn't important, too."

Jasmine appreciated his reassurance. She hadn't realized the trace of envy that had crept in when she'd spoken to her friend. Envy, and the worst emotion of all, self-doubt. The call had come on a day when the house she'd photographed was nothing more than dilapidated wood that barely stood. She'd wondered if anyone would care about the family who'd lived and thrived there.

"Thank you," she said. "A part of me knows I wouldn't have the opportunity to do this if someone didn't think the stories were worth telling. Another part of me wonders if I should have just stuck with fashion photography and left the important work to others."

"It doesn't matter if you're taking pictures of homes or supermodels, your work is important. Everyone has a job to do. How you do that job is a reflection of your character. You care about these untold stories, therefore, you're the person who should be telling them."

"Dang, did you ever consider becoming a motivational speaker? You've certainly made me feel better."

He chuckled. "Maybe I'll fall back on that if this broadcasting thing doesn't work out."

"I go back to New York in a few weeks. That's when I'll decide on the actual photos I want to display."

"I look forward to seeing them," he said.

Did that mean he expected them to be together even after the summer ended? If so, why wouldn't he tell her the real reason he was retiring? Why introduce her to his friends and talk about taking her to Milan to celebrate if he didn't want them to move forward?

Stop being ridiculous and ask him.

Kevin's cell phone rang before she could make up her mind about having the conversation or not.

"Incoming call from Sabrina," stated the monotone voice of his SUV's Bluetooth interface.

"Accept," Kevin said.

Jasmine barely kept her jaw from dropping. He was going to answer his ex-wife's call with her in the car? She would have expected him to not want her to over-hearing anything. Julio got upset if she even asked about a conversation with his ex-wife. Did that mean Kevin trusted her to hear? That there wasn't anything poten-tially incriminating for her to overhear?

Or did it mean Jasmine was so insignificant when

it came to the relationship he had with Sabrina that it didn't matter what she heard?

And there you go borrowing trouble.

"Sabrina, hey, on speaker in my car and I've got someone with me," Kevin answered.

Well, that answered most of her questions. He'd referred to her ambivalently as "someone," which was neither important nor unimportant. Sabrina would know anything she said would be overheard and therefore that left the ball in her court as to how comfy the conversation got.

"Okay, this will only take a few minutes anyway," Sabrina responded. Her voice was husky and smooth. The kind of voice Jasmine imagined would keep men up at night with all kinds of sexy dreams.

That Sabrina didn't ask who the "someone" in the car was answered another question. Kevin routinely answered her calls with other people around and Sabrina didn't care enough to find out who listened in.

"Okay, shoot," he said.

"Are you getting Asia's gift for her birthday? I'm trying to get all of the details for her party together and I want to be sure you won't drop the ball." Sabrina's voice, sexy huskiness aside, was tight, a little frazzled and slightly accusatory.

Kevin's shoulders tightened, but he chuckled and shook his head, clearly a little bothered by his ex-wife's state. "Calm, down, kitten, I told you I'd handle the gift and I've got it."

There was that nickname again. Jasmine pulled her hand out of Kevin's. He shot her a glance, but she looked out of the window instead.

"Are you sure? This is going to be a huge surprise.

I've promised her and her friends that the party will be fantastic."

"Have I let you or her down before?"

"Do you really want to go there?" Sabrina snapped.

Kevin took a slow breath. "I haven't missed a birthday party since Paris was three. Come on, Sabrina, you know I've got this." He still sounded calm, but there was an undertone of frustration and disappointment. "I promise I'll be there and Asia will have the best sweet sixteen party. Jacobe is friends with Dante Wilson and Raymond. I confirmed with Raymond on the phone yesterday. He will be at her party and will sing happy birthday."

Sabrina's relieved sigh echoed through the car. "Okay, I just want to be sure."

"Trust me, okay?" His tone was reassuring, but why did he have to dip into the warm and fuzzy territory that had made Jasmine's heart melt? Now it made her stomach churn. There was definitely something with him and the ex.

"I will. Just…don't forget to call me if *anything* changes. I'll talk with you soon."

The call ended. Silence filled the car. "You want to tell me why you're all stiff now?"

"I'm not stiff," Jasmine replied.

"Yes, you are. What's the deal? What did I say?"

Jasmine shifted and faced him. The lights outside were less frequent as they entered a more secluded residential area. "You two still seem really close."

"We are close. We've got two kids." His voice was easy, calm, infuriating.

"You call her kitten."

He frowned, then his face cleared up and he laughed.

"Yeah, that's an old habit. Sabrina is kind of high-strung. She's always been that way. When she gets mad, she's ready to scratch everyone's eyes out. In high school, everyone said she fought like an alley cat. I started calling her kitten to show her I wasn't afraid of her attitude. It works if I keep an easy tone and no sudden movements. She eventually calms down and comes around. It doesn't mean anything."

"It sounds like it means something." She hated the jealous sound of her voice, but she was jealous. Maybe they were just *having fun* and jealousy shouldn't play in their situation, but jealousy wasn't an emotion that tended to follow the rules.

Kevin took her hand back and brought it to his mouth again. "I promise there's nothing more there. Sabrina and I had our time and it didn't work. She's engaged now. I'm happy for her. It's nothing."

"She's engaged?"

"Getting married in six months."

"And you're okay with that?" She watched for any signs of jealousy. Just like she knew she shouldn't be jealous of his ex but couldn't help herself, he may be going through the same thing. If that were the case, it was a hard no for her. This would end immediately.

"Why wouldn't I be? I have no claim on Sabrina and she has no claim on me. As long as he treats her and my kids well, I don't care who she marries. I don't love her anymore." His voice was steady, sure. No eye twitches, stiff shoulders or uncomfortable shifting. She believed him.

"Why does she think you'll mess up the birthday plans?"

He didn't answer for several seconds. His shoulders were tight. "After our divorce, I partied a lot. One party started in Vegas and ended in Dubai. I missed our daughter's third birthday. I was supposed to have brought the cake."

"That must have been some party." It was all she could think to say.

The corner of his mouth tilted up and some tension left his shoulders. "It was. It was also the moment I realized just because I was divorced, it didn't mean I could be an absentee father. I won't let my kids down ever again. Not if I can help it."

"How old is Paris now?"

"Twelve."

"She's still holding that against you and it was nine years ago?"

"I wish that was the only time I screwed up after our divorce, but it was the last. Trust takes a long time to regain. If dealing with her expectation that I'll disappoint the girls helps keep us cool, I'll deal. Not being a part of my kids' lives isn't happening."

He pulled down a drive that she hadn't seen from the road. She thought about his words while he maneuvered down the winding road. So Sabrina was getting married. That was good. The pet name explanation made sense, too.

Sabrina's expectation that Kevin would always be a disappointment was a little disheartening. Despite the media reports on his wild lifestyle, Jasmine had seen for herself that family was the most important thing to him. He'd saved his hometown because his mom and grandmother still lived there. He obviously loved his kids and had made his blended family work.

You weren't there. You don't know their history.

True, but she was learning about the man he was today. She couldn't imagine Kevin turning his back on his family or ignoring their needs.

She placed her hand over his. "You're getting Raymond to sing at your daughter's birthday party. That has to be the best thing ever."

He relaxed and grinned. "He's her favorite singer. I hope it's not too much."

"Believe me, she's going to love it. You'll be crowned father of the year."

A large home overlooking the river came into view. He parked next to the other luxury vehicles lined in front of the house. He got out of the car and came up to her side. Once he opened the door for her, he helped her down and pulled her directly into his arms. The kiss he laid on her lips snatched the air from her lungs. Her breasts suddenly felt heavy. Her body hummed for more.

"Don't ever think I want to go backward. There is only one woman I want, and she's in my arms right now. You got that?" His voice was low and solid. His eyes burned with a flame that made her want to drag him into the back seat and finish that make-out-like-teens session they'd had earlier.

"I got it." Her voice came out deep and throaty.

He nodded. "Good." He took her by the hand and led her to the door of the huge house. She recognized Isaiah Reynolds, player for the Jacksonville Gators, when he answered the door. He and Kevin greeted each other with one-arm hugs and backslaps.

"Kevin, I was hoping you would drop in for couples game night." Isaiah grinned at them, an eager and pleased expression on his face.

Couples game night? Kevin had invited her to couples game night? Oh shit, that was relationship status.

"This is my girl, Jasmine," Kevin said by way of answer. "Jasmine, this is Isaiah, the guy we're going to embarrass at game night."

Jasmine laughed and tightened her grip on Kevin's hand. The smile on her face made her cheeks ache. She'd explore the happy feelings bursting in her later. For now, she was going to enjoy the night.

"Nice to meet you, Isaiah. Sorry in advance for the beatdown."

Chapter 16

A month after the couples game night, Jasmine found herself smiling from ear to ear when the car dropped her off at Kevin's condo in Atlanta. Worries about their relationship status hadn't plagued her since the night he'd introduced her to his closest friends and their significant others. They hadn't had "the talk" about where things were going, but when he'd called her sister to ask what dessert he could surprise her with for her birthday dinner that wouldn't cause too much of an issue with her diabetes, Jasmine had taken that as a sign they were officially dating.

When Kevin opened the door to his condo, her greeting stuck in her throat. Who the hell was this handsome man, and how was she supposed to focus on anything but getting the perfectly tailored navy suit off his body? She'd never seen Kevin in a suit. They'd gone out when they met up on weekends, but mostly for casual, low-key dates or fun outings. She'd seen him in a suit on television in post-game interviews, but not up close and personal. He looked damn fine in a suit.

Kevin looked down at his clothes and ran a hand over his tie. His eyes were confused when they met hers again. "What's wrong? Is there something on my suit?"

She shook her head. "No. You just look—" she grinned "—really good."

Tension seeped out of his shoulders and he stepped back so she could enter. As soon as she crossed the threshold, he took the overnight bag from her hand and pulled her into his embrace. "You look really good, too."

His kiss immediately heated her blood. Jasmine dropped her purse to the floor and wrapped her arm around his neck. His body was solid steel beneath the fine material of his suit.

Two weeks had passed since they'd last spent a weekend together. Two weeks of sexting, late-night phone conversations and trying to bridge the sexual gap on her own. Now that she was here in his arms, with his body pressed against hers and his kiss intensifying with each passing second, she wanted him to slam her against the wall and take the edge off.

She put just enough distance between them to work at the button of his jacket.

"I've got a meeting," Kevin said. His hand covered hers at his jacket, but he didn't stop kissing her.

"You're going to have to be late," she said.

He groaned, low and throaty. "Damn, Jasmine, you make me want to forget everything."

She cupped the rigid length of him through his pants. "Then forget everything."

His hand gripped her ass. "I can't." He eased back

to give her soft, gentle kisses. Didn't he know what those did to her?

"Why?" Damn, was that her voice coming out pleading and breathless? She rubbed her breasts against his chest.

"Because…" he started. Jasmine massaged him through his pants. "Shit, that feels good."

"Dad, do you have any more soda?" a young girl's voice came from the back of the house.

A naked dip in the Arctic Ocean wouldn't have frozen Jasmine any faster. Her head fell back and she met Kevin's gaze. "One of your kids is here?" She kept her voice low.

"I was going to tell you that," he whispered back. "Look in the pantry," he called toward the back of the house.

"Okay," came the response.

"What's going on?" Jasmine eased out of his embrace.

"It's Asia. Sabrina went to Orlando with Paris for a math competition," Kevin explained, referring to his second daughter. "Asia didn't want to go, so I agreed to watch her. Sabrina was supposed to be back before you got here, but their flight was delayed. I couldn't exactly kick her out even though I knew you were coming. I was going to see about dropping her off at a friend's until Sabrina got back, but then Clive called and said the executives with Taylor Sports wants to meet right now. I can take her with me. I know your thing with kids."

Yeah, her thing with kids. Not getting too attached. Not meeting them unless the relationship was going somewhere. Old fear made her want to call back her Lyft driver and say she'd meet up with Kevin after he handled everything. New hope that she and Kevin could make a relationship work kept her feet planted on the floor.

Jasmine pointed toward the back of the house. "Don't do that. We can hang out until you're done."

He stilled and raised a brow. "I thought you didn't do kids."

"I didn't say that." She didn't do kids with a guy she didn't want to fall in love with. Too late for that. She'd fallen for Kevin. "I said I don't like kids forced on me, but you're in a tough spot. I know this thing with Taylor Sports is a big deal. I'm happy to hang with her for a few hours until you get things settled. No biggie." She gave him what she hoped was a no-biggie smile.

This was *not* a no-biggie situation. When she'd met his younger kids, that had been accidental. She wasn't the woman he was sleeping with when that happened. She'd just been the photographer talking to his grandmother. That could easily be written off.

This. This was completely different. Purposefully hanging out with his daughter when they were officially a couple was a legit introduction. This was real relationship stuff.

Kevin put his hand at the small of her back and guided her toward the back of the house. "I already told her about the meeting. She's excited for me to go. I told her you were coming, and she actually wants to meet you."

"You told her about me?"

"Why wouldn't I? You were coming over and her mom's flight is delayed. There's a good chance she would have met you anyway." He said it in that same no-biggie tone she'd used earlier.

Kevin took her straight to the kitchen where a tall,

young girl poured soda into a glass filled with ice. She looked up and grinned when she saw them. There were braces on her teeth. Her curly hair was pulled up in a giant puff on the top of her head. She had Kevin's smile and complexion.

"Asia, this is Jasmine," Kevin introduced them. His voice was expectant. His body a little stiff.

Jasmine lifted a hand and waved awkwardly. "Hey, Asia."

Asia's grin widened. "Oh my God, you two are so cute! Dad, you didn't tell me she had blue hair. I want blue hair!"

Kevin's body relaxed. "No blue hair until your mom agrees with it."

Asia huffed, but then her smile came back out with full brightness. "Fine. Hey, Jasmine, want to go to the mall while Dad's at his meeting?"

"Uh…sure," Jasmine stammered a little, stunned by Asia's quick acquiescence to hanging with her dad's new girlfriend. Did Kevin introduce a lot of his girl-friends to his kids? Was she reading into things? "Anything you're looking for in particular?"

"Not really. I usually shop online and hate the mall, but they're having this big promotion at Sephora. Free lip gloss with each purchase. I figured it wouldn't hurt to check it out."

"I'm cool with that." She looked at Kevin. "That cool with you?"

He nodded. "Fine with me. Grab something to eat while you're out. When I'm done with this meeting, I'll see where you two are at and we can hook up and do something until Sabrina gets back."

He crossed the kitchen and kissed Asia on the top of her head. "Don't talk Jasmine's ear off."

"I'll try not to," Asia said in a voice that said she'd do the opposite.

Kevin laughed and picked up a set of keys. He crossed to Jasmine and kissed her cheek. "I'll try and make this quick."

"No rush. We'll be fine." Her tone was cheerful, even though her heart hammered and she felt thrown off balance.

"Thank you so much for this," he said. Appreciation was a warm caress in his voice.

She smiled her *you're welcome*. He kissed her again and then was gone. Jasmine glanced back at Asia. "So…"

Asia held up a hand. "Hey, just one thing. My dad deserves to be happy. I want him to be happy and I think you make him happy. Are you really into him or are you just trying to take advantage of him?"

The bluntness threw Jasmine for a second. Any thought to tell Asia to mind her business was washed away by the protectiveness in the girl's voice. She obviously didn't want anyone to hurt her dad.

"I care about your dad. A lot."

Asia nodded. The bright smile returned. "Good. He needs that. Even though I don't think he thinks he does." She picked up her glass and walked toward the door. "I'm going to get my stuff and we can go. I can't wait to hear all about you. My dad's got a girlfriend. Finally!" Asia lifted her shoulders and squealed before prancing out of the kitchen.

Jasmine forced her mouth to close. Guess that answered the question about girlfriends meeting his kids. She bit her lower lip to hold back the grin. She was Kevin's girlfriend.

* * *

Kevin hated when people whistled a tune. The sound of whistling usually made his neck tighten, made him want to tell the offender to find another way to express their giddiness. He could never think of anything good enough to warrant whistling. That was until today. He whistled his own cheery tune as he entered his condo.

Finally, things were going right for him. The meeting with Taylor Sports had gone better than expected. They wanted his outgoing personality, as they'd expressed it, to mix things up on their current basketball broadcast show. Despite being one of the oldest players in the league, they felt Kevin would bring a "youthful point of view" compared to the retired players who'd been champions years ago.

On-screen interviews were still required, but the job was basically his for the taking. And he was going to take it. The idea of doing something different without having to completely leave the game behind eased the pain of retirement. He felt useful again.

On top of that, Asia had given Jasmine a glowing review. He'd gotten the text from Sabrina that her plane landed and she and Paris were on the way home. He and Jasmine and Asia had had a late lunch after his meeting, he'd dropped Jasmine back at his place, and then he'd taken taking Asia home. Her shopping trip with Jasmine had been a success—yielding the free lip gloss and apparently a new sparkly eyeliner. She'd given Jasmine a teenager's highest honor, the label of cool.

"She's cool, Dad," Asia had said before getting out of the car at her mom's house. "I think you'll be happy with her."

Paris's group had placed in the math competition,

so when Kevin had walked Asia inside, they'd focused on celebrating his daughter's good news. He'd left after promising to take Paris to the next superhero film coming out the following Friday.

He hadn't realized he wanted his kids' approval. He'd never introduced any of his kids to the women he dated because their approval wasn't needed. The women he'd seen in the past hadn't been likely to become anything more than a random hookup with little chance of a deep connection. That's what he'd thought would happen with him and Jasmine, but over the summer, things had slowly morphed into more than that.

Was he ready for a serious relationship? No. She still didn't know about his body breaking down. History proved he couldn't give the type of commitment expected in a relationship. He'd never failed in his career. Never not gotten something he really wanted. The job offer with Taylor Sports was another example. But he failed at relationships.

He didn't want to fail with Jasmine, but what happened a year, two or three years from now when the pain got worse? When the demands of his job took up more of his time?

What if he grew bored and the excitement of being involved in television lured him away the same way the new fame of being a professional athlete had lured him before? Would Jasmine tell him he wasn't there for her the same way Hanna had? Would he walk away because he couldn't handle the pressure to be the perfect partner like he had with Sabrina?

His whistling ended when he walked into the condo. The sound of jazz drifted from his living area accompanied by Jasmine's voice humming to the music.

He shoved thoughts of the future out of his mind. Right now was what mattered. He'd won the job. His kids were happy. He had a beautiful woman waiting for him in his home. To hell with the future.

Jasmine sat on the floor next to his coffee table, her camera in her hands as she studied the screen. She'd changed into a T-shirt and shorts. The smell of her bodywash, a crisp citrus scent imprinted on his brain, filled the space. She must have showered. Which meant that sweet scent was all over her body, ready for him to explore. His body hardened.

"What are you working on?" he asked.

She glanced up from her camera. "Looking at the pictures I took before coming to Atlanta. Asia was interested when I told her about my project. I haven't gone through them yet to see which ones I'd like to have for the showing."

Kevin tugged off his tie and unbuttoned the top of his shirt. "How do you like them?"

"It's hard to pick my favorites, but I think that's because I'm so into this project. Every angle captures the history of these places along with the loss of that history over time. It's sad."

"Not anymore," he said. He sat on the arm of the couch. "You're bringing that history back to life. That's a good thing."

Her smile punched him in the chest. Damn, coming home and having her smile at him like that after a good day would be better than winning the playoffs. A bad day would be bearable knowing she was there waiting to smile at him.

"You're right," she said. "Which makes picking the

best pictures even harder." She sucked in her lower lip and studied her camera.

He pulled his jacket off and tossed it on the couch. She slid her lip from between her teeth. It was plump, swollen and wet. Images of slipping her lip between his teeth filled his mind. Running his hands over her curves. Making other parts of her body wet and swollen.

Kevin spread his legs to accommodate his growing erection. "Focus on something else for a while."

"Like what?" Jasmine glanced up at him. She must have seen something in his expression because her smoky eyes darkened with desire.

He unbuttoned the rest of his shirt. Her hungry gaze followed the movement with an intensity that felt like a caress. She lifted a brow and licked that delectable lower lip, accelerating his heart rate with the movement. He loved when she looked at him as if she couldn't wait to run her tongue over his body.

"I can think of a few things for you to focus on instead of that camera," he replied.

"I think I want to play with the camera a little longer." She lifted the camera to her eye. Snapped a photo of him.

Kevin raised a brow. "You've got plenty of pictures of me."

"None where you look this tempting," she answered, her voice husky with promise.

He liked that answer. He slipped out of his shirt. "Tempting, huh? I thought I was pretty tempting the first day we met."

"You were very tempting then." She snapped another picture. "But that was work. This is for fun."

Kevin slid from the arm of the chair to the seat. He

leaned back and popped the button of his slacks. She sucked in a breath. Raising an eyebrow, he eased down the zipper. The sound vibrated and pulsed through the room, the sultry beat of jazz the perfect backdrop to this game of foreplay.

He slowly slid a hand into the waistband of his underwear. "How much fun do you want to have?"

Jasmine's heart pounded harder with each snap of her camera. She'd never forget Kevin's naked body. The works of art that canvased his skin. The strength and agility apparent in every muscle on his body.

No, the vision of Kevin naked wasn't something she expected to fade quickly or easily. This was different.

For him to be willing to trust her to photograph him in the nude again. No room full of people, no staged shots to show off his athletic ability. Just him, her and the camera. That level of trust made her breasts heavy, her nipples hard and a deep need settle heavily between her thighs.

"I want to have a lot of fun," she told him.

She lifted the camera to her eye. Kevin stood, removed the rest of his clothes, then lowered back on the couch.

Jasmine's hands trembled, her breathing as erratic as the saxophone solo in the music. Wild, pulsing and soaring with passion infused in each breath. He was amazingly beautiful. Powerful and sleek in a way that made her want to melt into a pool of estrogen at his feet.

"You guide the shot, Jasmine," he said.

"Act as if I'm not here."

"That's the thing. When you're not here, I'm thinking

of you. Wishing you were here. Then I spend the night thinking about what would happen if you were here."

Something tightened in her chest. Those words were a lot more than sweet nothings. They rang with sincerity and the need she felt whenever she was away from him. "Then what do you do when you think of me?"

The smile on his face was decadent. A smile that made her squirm on the floor and ease forward with her camera to capture the sinful twist of his lips.

"This." His voice was rough and tight. Long fingers wrapped around his length. Kevin showed her exactly what he did when she wasn't there.

Keeping the camera in her hand became difficult as her palms dampened with sweat. Her body shivered. He was so damn hot. So damn sexy and tempting. Open and raw without a bit of shyness or hesitation in front of her or the camera. Kevin didn't do anything in halves, including driving her crazy just by touching himself.

Jasmine put down the camera and crawled across the floor to him. His head was thrown back, eyes closed and lips parted with heavy breaths. She placed her hands on his knees. He didn't jerk. Just opened his eyes to stare at her and smile as if he knew she wouldn't be able to resist him and stay on the other side of the room.

She pushed his hand aside and took over his work. That turned his smug look into one of complete surrender.

"Damn, Jasmine, I love your hands on me."

Her grip on him firmed. When her lips caressed him in a soft kiss, his body went rigid. He sat up, swept her onto her feet and over his shoulder.

"Kevin! What are you doing?"

"If you do that, this won't last long." His strides were

long and determined. They reached the bedroom in a flash and then she was on her back on the bed.

He wasn't gentle as he jerked her clothes off. The urgency of his movements created a sense of frenzy in her. Her hands touched and caressed every part of him she could reach. She knew her touches were driving him just as crazy. His drive to get her naked and against him made her want to take him to the pinnacle of pleasure.

He nearly pulled the top drawer of his nightstand completely out when he jerked it open and pulled out a condom. The foil wrapping didn't last. He was covered and pushing into her with the quick agility she'd marveled at in his muscles.

His fingers dug into her hip as he pinned her down with one hand. The other braced above her head. He drove into her with fierce, determined strokes. "You drive me crazy. Do you feel what you do to me?"

Feel it? She loved it. She nodded, maybe moaned something and grabbed onto his arms as he pushed her over the edge.

His hand tightened. He pulled back. Made her whimper at the loss. Plunged deep. "Do you feel that?"

"Oh God, I love that," she moaned.

"You love that, huh?" His voice was a sensual caress to her senses. He repeated the movement. Her body clenched around him. Taking the pleasure.

"Yes." Her head pushed back into the mattress.

He lowered and kissed her ear. The long strokes melding into a slow grind made her toes curl. "Tell me that you love it. Tell me that you want it. Tell me, Jasmine."

His body pressed against her sensitive nub as he loved her with full, deep strokes. She wanted him.

Couldn't think about anyone else when they were apart. Couldn't imagine not talking to him again. Not feeling him against her again. Her body exploded with the force of her orgasm.

Her nails dug into his back. "Ahh, Kevin, God, I love you!"

His body shivered, jerked, and he followed her over the edge. Her eyes popped open. The afterglow of being thoroughly made love to by Kevin was erased by what she'd said.

Holy fucking shit!

It wasn't a lie. She loved him.

Kevin didn't hold her like he typically did afterward. He pulled away carefully. Avoided eye contact as he rolled off the bed and mumbled, "I've got to clean up."

Jasmine's heart plummeted to the center of the Earth. She'd committed the ultimate just-having-fun faux pas. She'd told Kevin she loved him when he obviously didn't love her back.

Chapter 17

She loved him.

That was not how this was supposed to go. At all. The sex was great. Freaking fantastic! The conversation was good. His friends and one of four kids had signed off on her, but they were still just chilling. They weren't going to put undue expectations on what was happening between them. She wasn't supposed to say *I love you*!

That changed every damn thing.

Maybe it was in-the-moment sex talk. Instead of saying, *I love this*, or *I love it*, she'd accidentally said *you*.

Yeah right.

Was her loving him really a bad thing? He liked her. Cared about her even. He looked forward to seeing her, and, again, the sex was amazing. Maybe her loving him wouldn't be a bad thing.

Her loving you means she's going to want this to be defined. A relationship.

Love meant forever. Love meant expectations of

marriage. Love meant *I'm trusting you with my heart so don't screw up and break the damn thing*. He wasn't ready for that. Just when he was getting used to the idea of maybe doing the *let's try this couple thing*, she had to go and say *I love you* and ruin everything.

Love! He was a failure at love. No better than his dad.

Kevin cringed at his reflection in the bathroom mirror. This was bad because now he'd see the look of disappointment and pain in her eyes that he'd seen twice before, and sooner than expected. He was bound to see it when he told her he wasn't ready for love to enter into what they were doing.

He hadn't been able to love Sabrina or Hanna the way they'd wanted to be loved. He'd loved Sabrina with all the fierce emotion that came with a first love, but that hadn't been enough to make him want to spend the rest of his life with her once he'd gotten out of Silver Springs and seen more of the world. Now he loved her as the mother of his kids, but knew he could never give her what she wanted.

Then there was Hanna. Hanna who had been the perfect mistress. They'd enjoyed each other's company without any expectations. Then the pregnancy had come, followed by the twins and he'd figured he'd have to be in love because she was having his children. She'd walked away a year later.

You don't love me, Kevin. I can't stick around and wait for you to love me.

He wasn't made for long-term. He hated hurting the people who cared about him. He couldn't bear to see Jasmine's love for him eventually turn into hate.

There was a knock on the bathroom door. Kevin

took a deep breath and opened it. Jasmine, naked and beautiful, stood on the other side.

"You plan to hide in there all night?" she tried to tease, but worry clouded her gaze.

Shit, she had meant the words. Which meant he had to say something back. *Hey, thanks for your love, but don't expect it in return* probably wasn't what she wanted to hear.

"I was just about to come out."

"Hey, about that." She pointed over her shoulder toward the bed. "About what I said. Let's not make it a big deal."

A mixture of relief and disappointment washed over him. The relief he got. The disappointment…that was unexpected. He focused on the relief. She didn't want to make what she said a big deal. She wasn't really in love with him. That was good. He didn't want love to come up in their relationship. Regardless, of the damn knot forming in his chest.

"I'm not," he infused his voice with an extra bit of don't-be-silly and punctuated it with a shoulder shrug. "Stuff said during sex doesn't mean anything."

Her brows drew together. "It doesn't?"

"Yeah, everyone says crazy things when they're having sex." He kissed her forehead. "I didn't give it a second thought."

He walked past her into the bedroom, the lie harder to tell than he'd expected. He'd just freaked about her falling in love with him, but now that she was taking it back, a sense of unease settled around him. Why? He didn't love her.

You're not acting like a guy who isn't in love.

He shut up the inner critic.

"So…you don't have any feelings about what I said?"

"Only glad that we're on the same page," he answered, keeping his back to her.

His cell phone rang. He'd left it in the living room and took that as the escape plan he needed. He strode out of the room. His phone was in the pocket of his pants on the floor. By the time he dug it out, the call had ended. He checked the caller ID. Sabrina. Frowning, he dialed back.

"Kevin?" Sabrina snapped.

"Yeah, I couldn't get to the phone in time."

She scoffed. "Let me guess—you're busy with your latest fling?"

"What are you talking about?" He immediately went on the defensive against her accusatory tone.

"Asia told me you introduced her to one of your playthings. What the hell, Kevin? We agreed that you wouldn't bring those women around the kids."

"Hold up, I didn't bring one of *those women* around. Jasmine was in town and I had a meeting last minute. She was only with Asia for a few hours."

"She took our daughter shopping," Sabrina slowly enunciated each word, judgment and anger an extra pinch on each word. "Now Asia is talking about her dad's new girlfriend who's so great with her piercings and blue hair. She's already telling her sister that there's going to be a wedding."

Kevin stumbled back a few steps. The words felt like a blow to the stomach. "Wait…what? That's crazy. There isn't going to be a wedding."

"I know that. That's why we came up with the rules. No introducing them to the women you're *sleeping* with. They're itching for you to settle down, Kevin. You can't bring your women around all the time. It gets the girls' hopes up."

"Look, I'll talk to Asia. Jasmine and I are cool, but it's not that serious," Kevin explained.

"Then you shouldn't have brought her around Asia in the first place," Sabrina snapped. She took a breath as if calming herself. "You know the rule. Introduce her to the family first. You came up with this rule and I followed it when things got serious with Mac."

That had been his rule. With their blended family, none of them had wanted their kids to get attached to someone who was only in their lives for a fleeting moment. He'd heard too many horror stories of wannabe stepparents coming in and hurting kids. If things got serious, each parent was to know and meet the person who'd be around their kids.

Kevin pinched the bridge of his nose and sighed. "Look, I hear you, okay? I messed up and should have told you about Jasmine. I was in a bind with the meeting and I didn't think." He'd trusted Jasmine completely with Asia. "You can stop now. I'll talk with Asia and it won't happen again."

"See that it doesn't." The call ended.

Kevin swore. The entire conversation irritated him even more. He should have told Sabrina about Jasmine before he introduced her to Asia. He'd broken his own rule and he accepted that.

That wasn't the source of his irritation. Sabrina talking about Jasmine as if she were nothing bothered the crap out of him. Yes, he'd had a freak-out moment when he thought they were approaching the *I love you* portion of this relationship, but that didn't mean she was just like the other women he'd dated recently. Jasmine was different.

He went back into the bedroom. There was no way she hadn't heard his end of the conversation. Sabrina had been yelling and his voice had risen in response.

Jasmine wasn't in the bedroom. The bathroom door was closed. The sound of running water came from the other end.

He exhaled in relief. If she'd been in there and hadn't heard, at least they wouldn't have another awkward conversation about Sabrina being angry about Jasmine spending time with Asia today. He flipped off the overhead light, turned on the bedside lamp and slipped between the covers. The bathroom door opened, and Jasmine stopped in the door. Their gazes met. She looked away first.

She didn't say anything as she crossed the room and got into bed beside him. Kevin rolled over and pulled her back against his front. She didn't stiffen or fight the movement.

Everything seemed right but felt weird. Her blurted words, the quick sweeping of them under the rug, Sabrina's call. They all loomed over their heads like spiders.

"Good night, Jasmine," he said, pulling her closer and closing his eyes. Everything could wait until tomorrow.

She sighed. "Good night, Kevin."

Kevin jerked awake. His room was dark. His heart pounded with the adrenaline from being woken suddenly. He glanced to his left.

Jasmine wasn't in the bed with him. Odd.

He looked at the clock. They'd fallen asleep a few hours ago. The sun was still down, and the sky was dark outside his window. Where was she?

A rattling sound came from the kitchen. Frowning, Kevin threw back the covers and jumped out of the bed. He grabbed a pair of boxers from the drawer before going to investigate. When he got to the kitchen, his frown deepened.

Jasmine was in there. She was on her knees at the door of his pantry. Frantically, she pushed things aside and mumbled to herself.

"Jasmine, what are you doing?" He kept his voice calm so as not to startle her.

She jumped anyway. Flipping around to look at him and falling onto her rear. "Why are you sneaking up on me?"

"I heard a noise and you weren't in the bed. I came to look for you."

Her skin glowed under the kitchen lights with a fine sheen of sweat. "I feel myself going low. I came in here for a snack."

He immediately crossed the room to kneel beside her on the floor. He'd been with her on other nights when her blood sugar levels had gone low. She usually kept snacks or juice with her to bring her levels back up. He should have thought of that. "Are you okay? Do you need me to get you anything?"

She waved a hand. "No, I'm fine. I just had a hard time finding anything in here. I had planned to go to the store earlier and get some juice boxes but got distracted with Asia."

"I can go to the store if you need me to," he offered. Guilt pressed heavily on his chest. He'd asked her to stay with him, then hadn't thought about what she would need if she stayed the night.

Way to be a good boyfriend there, Kevin. Letting her down already and you haven't even claimed the official boyfriend title yet.

He pushed aside the critical thought.

She picked up the box next to her on the floor. "I found Pop-Tarts," she said triumphantly. "Half of one should be good." She opened the box and took out one of the strawberry pastries.

"You should have reminded me to stock up before you came. I would have." Self-reproach seeped into his voice making the words sharper than he'd intended.

She took a bite of the Pop-Tart. "I didn't think I'd have to tell you," she mumbled around the food in her mouth. She threw a judgmental glare his way.

Kevin sat on the floor and crossed his arms. "What?"

"I mean really, Kevin. How many nights have we spent together?" The words were slightly slurred. Her eyes narrowed.

Her levels must have gotten low. He'd seen this side of her, too. The cranky, not quite coherent Jasmine that came out when she needed insulin.

He reached for her hands to help her up. "We've spent several nights together." He kept his voice calm.

Jasmine jerked her hands out of his reach. "Yeah, and on the several nights we've spent together, I've gotten up a few times because I needed something."

"I'm aware of that."

"And you—" she pointed the half eaten Pop-Tart at him "—should have realized that and had things here."

He'd had the same thought earlier, but hearing the accusation from her lips put him on defense. "Whoa,

whoa, wait a second. I'll admit I could've stocked up knowing you were coming. But you've dealt with this all your life. I know you know how to take care of yourself."

He clenched his teeth to stop from saying more. When Jasmine got like this, it scared him. Scared him to see her personality and body become something other than the bright, vibrant person he cared for. He knew her condition wasn't her fault, but he hated knowing she was sick and there was little he could do.

"I guess I shouldn't have expected anything else. I mean, we aren't really in a relationship, are we? I'm nobody."

"Where the hell is this coming from?" He had a good idea.

She struggled to get up. Kevin moved fast, ignoring the stiffness in his knees and arms to help her up.

"I heard you on the phone, Kevin." She jerked her arms out of his grip when she was on her feet. "You told your ex-wife I wasn't important to you."

"I told her Asia was setting high expectations, but I didn't say you weren't important to me."

"You said we weren't getting married."

He tried to tamp back his frustration. "Because we aren't."

"Are you saying you never want to marry me?" she asked, affronted.

"Hold up, you just told me you loved me, then took it back. Now you want to talk about marriage?" Maybe reasoning with her right now wasn't the best thing, but his mind whirled at the hurt in her voice.

"I took it back because I didn't want you to freak out."

"Who said I was going to freak out?"

She poked him in the chest. "You disappeared in the bathroom after I said it. That's a freak-out. What was I supposed to say after that?"

"The truth."

Her eyes widened as if the idea of being truthful hadn't occurred to her. She regained her composure, nodded with quick, jerky movements and straightened her shoulders. "Okay, fine, here's the truth. I do love you. There. Happy now?"

Kevin cringed and then pinched the bridge of his nose. It was too late, and he was too tired for this. She wasn't feeling well and, as he'd seen previously, may not remember this conversation tomorrow. "Jasmine, you don't know what you're saying."

"Oh, first it was sex made me say it. Now it's my need for a Pop-Tart." She threw the rest of the pastry on the floor. It broke into several dry pieces.

"Well, you aren't always logical when you get like this."

"I'm perfectly logical," she said in a cool, clear voice. "I need something to keep me from going low. That doesn't mean I don't know what I'm saying or that I won't remember this in the morning, or that I won't remember what you say or don't say tomorrow."

"What I *don't* say?"

She took a step toward him, her dark eyes intent. The colorful scarf she'd put around her hair was loose enough for the blue tips of her hair to slip out. "Just admit it. You freaked when I told you I loved you. You don't love me and you don't want to marry me."

He didn't want to say it. Saying so would mean the end of them, and he wasn't ready for the end of them. "Jasmine, I care about you. What we've got going is fine. Why do you want to have this discussion now?"

A sheen covered her eyes. "Because eventually I'll want those things you don't want to define. I want someone who loves me. Possibly get married one day. I want a guy who cares enough to think about me coming into town, who puts juice boxes in the pantry."

She wanted more than just juice boxes in the pantry. She wanted to depend on him. Trust that he'd be the man she needed. The partner in her life who she could always count on to be there. The kind of man he'd failed to be. "I told you I'm not good with that."

"Why aren't you good with that? Because you're divorced? News flash, sometimes people get divorced but that doesn't mean they can't fall in love again."

"Yeah, well, I tried that, too, and it didn't work out," he snapped back. "She said I couldn't love her. That I wasn't there for her. And when she walked out after having the twins, I realized the only thing I cared about were the twins. Not that I was losing her. I can't give you what you want. I'm not capable of that."

"Maybe they weren't right for you."

"There is no such thing as the right one. The only thing those kinds of thoughts lead to are expectations and disappointment. I don't want to disappoint you."

"You already have." She tried to push past him.

Kevin took her arm and pulled her close. She struggled to get out of his hold. He didn't let go. Tonight was a fluke. They'd talk tomorrow, work things out. Keep this going a little longer.

"Jasmine, chill."

"I'm leaving."

"No you're not." He held her tighter. She didn't struggle, just leaned closer to him.

"You don't love me," she mumbled against his chest.

He cupped the back of her head. "I care about you a lot." More than he'd expected.

"I want more than that, Kevin. I can't stick around and keep doing this when this isn't what I want. Not for the long-term."

She leaned more heavily into him. He glanced at the remains of the Pop-Tart on the floor. She'd eaten about half before tossing it. She should be okay for the night. "Look, let's get some rest and talk in the morning. You're not feeling well and it's late. We've got the weekend to spend together."

"Tomorrow won't change how I feel."

A few more hours would give him time to think about what he wanted. Did he want to try to give her what she wanted? Was he ready to try again?

He lifted her up into his arms. His joints ached. He squeezed her tighter. Biting his lip as sweat popped along his brow. A few seconds later and he had his bearings.

Try to be what she needs when you can barely lift her? What if she gets really sick? What good would you be?

Jasmine's head rested on his shoulder. She sighed and relaxed into his body.

"We'll worry about tomorrow when it comes," he said.

He took her into the bedroom and laid her on the bed as gently as his stiff, aching joints would allow. Jasmine didn't notice his struggle. She sighed and rolled over. Her eyes drifted closed. Kevin pulled the covers over her, then slipped into the bed next to her. He wanted to pull her into the circle of his arms, but he also worried he'd stiffen up and feel worse in the morning.

Kevin reached a hand over and placed it on her hip.

Maybe he wouldn't break her heart. Maybe he could let go and love her. But how could he be the one to watch over her every night?

Chapter 18

The sound of music playing in another room woke Jasmine. She stretched and glanced around. Kevin wasn't in bed next to her, but the thought of him made her smile.

Then the memories of the day before pierced her brain with the unpleasantness of a roaring hangover. She'd had fun with Asia. Kevin had joined them, and they'd had more fun together, almost like Jasmine was part of the family. She'd liked that so much, she'd realized she loved him and wanted to be a part of his family.

And that's where the night began its downward spiral, great camera moment and lovemaking after excluded.

Falling in love was the dumb stuff she was supposed to have avoided this time. She wasn't supposed to fall in love with the guy and his kids again. Especially when the guy in question admitted he didn't want long-term commitments.

Then she'd been really dumb and screamed out that she loved him during sex. What type of cliché, over-the-top, I've-lost-my-mind foolishness was that?

Jasmine slapped her hand over her face and groaned. That should have been the highlight of her embarrassment. But no, the Jasmine-isn't-important-to-me conversation he'd had with his ex-wife had really taken the cake.

Asia didn't need to get overly excited about her dad being in a relationship. He had no intentions of ever marrying this woman. She'd just happened to be in town. No big deal at all.

What was she still doing here? She should have broken this off at the start of the summer. One and done was what they'd agreed to. Just a little bit of fun until they both left town. Instead she'd continued to meet up with him. Continued to accept his phone calls. Continued to believe that the little bones he threw to keep her attached were enough.

Well, they weren't. She wasn't about to find herself looking foolish again. The time had come to take care of herself and get out.

She pushed the covers back and went into the bathroom. After taking care of her needs, she showered, brushed her teeth and took her insulin. She was stalling, but her foolish heart insisted on it. For a few minutes longer, she wanted to pretend as if she and Kevin were in a real relationship. Not this friends-with-benefits-weekend-booty-call thing they'd started.

When she entered the kitchen several minutes later, she took a deep breath and prepared to tell Kevin that she wasn't sure about doing this anymore. She stopped in her tracks and frowned.

Kevin stood by the sink. An orange prescription bottle in his hand. His face was lined with frustration as he tried, unsuccessfully, to open the top. She'd been on the receiving end of a stubborn medicine bottle before, but Kevin seemed to be going through more than that. His hands looked stiff and awkward.

"Damn," he hissed and threw down the bottle. It hit the bottom of the sink in a loud clang.

Jasmine rushed across the room. "Let me help with that."

Kevin jumped and faced her. "You're up. I made breakfast." He slid in front of the sink.

"Kevin, what's going on?"

"Nothing. Coffee?" He avoided eye contact and rubbed the back of his neck.

"Stop telling me nothing," she snapped.

"I got frustrated because I couldn't get the bottle open. No big deal," he said.

"That was more than frustration. Let me help. I can open it for you." She reached around him for the bottle.

Kevin turned and snatched it up before she could get to it, but he moved too fast and the bottle slipped out of his hands. It hit the floor and slid away from him.

"You know what," she said, throwing her hands up. "Fine. You want to shut me out. I'll make it easy for you. I'm leaving." She turned to stalk back to the bedroom.

"Jasmine, I can't open the bottle."

She spun back to face him. "I think I saw that."

He ran a hand over his face. "No. I *can't* open it. My hands won't let me." The frustration was back in his voice. Frustration, anger, defeat.

Jasmine crossed to him. "What do you mean?"

He leaned back against the sink. "It's why I'm retiring. The real reason. I've had joint pain for years, but I ignored it. Played it off as just collateral damage from years of playing professional ball. When I almost cost us the playoff win, I knew it was more. I've got rheumatoid arthritis."

Jasmine's surprise was undercut with clarity. That explained so much. She'd noticed his stiff gait when he walked some times. The way he frowned at his hands whenever he talked about retiring. The reason why he would leave a game he loved so much when he was still young enough to play a few more seasons.

"Why didn't you tell me?"

He shrugged. "Pride. You met me because I was considered at the top of my game. One of the prime athletes out there. My body is taking that away from me. I didn't want you to think any less of me."

"That's the dumbest thing I've ever heard," she said, putting her hands on her hips.

His eyes snapped to hers. Surprise was etched into every muscle of his features. "What?"

"Kevin, I have Type I diabetes. My body fights itself on a daily basis. Don't you think I would understand?"

"I'm not who you thought I was."

"No, you're not." She said shaking her head. "Because I thought you were smarter than this. I thought you would realize that something like this wouldn't matter to me. I thought you would see that I would still be into you even with what you're going through."

"It isn't like that."

"Yes, it is like that. I guess I shouldn't be surprised. It's not like you ever pretended this wasn't just going to be a superficial relationship. Why tell me the truth when you only planned to sleep with me for a summer and move on?"

He reached for her. "Jasmine—"

She stepped back. Turning away, she went to the discarded bottle and picked it up. She twisted open the top. "Don't try to say something different. We both knew what this was."

She handed him the bottle.

"Jasmine, things are good. Why do you want to change up what we have?"

Spoken like a guy who wanted to keep getting laid without any expectations. "Look, I'm not asking you to marry me."

"Oh really? Because last night you were pretty upset about us not getting married." He slammed the prescription on the counter.

"Last night?" Then the rest hit her. Her where-is-this-going meltdown in the middle of her search for something to bring up her levels. "You told your wife I was nobody."

"My *ex*-wife! Dammit, Jasmine, I'm not Julio. Stop looking for excuses for me to get back with Sabrina."

The words punched her in the gut, robbing her of air and searing her body with pain. "I'm not looking for excuses."

In two strides, he was in front of her. "Yes you are. You think I don't see it? From the first day we met, you got weird whenever she called. You ran when you were first around my kids. You asked about my old nickname for her or how we were voted cutest couple twenty years ago. I'm not going back to her, but she and Hanna will always be in my life. We have kids. I wasn't a good husband, or boyfriend, but I'll be damned if I'm a bad father. They are always going to be in my life."

"I wouldn't expect you to not have them in your life."

"But would you also expect there to be a day when I went back to one of them?"

She opened her mouth to deny it but the words wouldn't come out.

He stepped back. Arms held wide. "You don't trust me."

"You make it hard when all you ever say is that you're terrible at relationships and you don't want to make us official. Even when we both felt things were changing. You can't tell me you didn't feel it. That you don't feel more for me than just lust."

Kevin placed his hands on the back of one of the chairs. "Because as soon as you put a name on something, things change. Why tempt fate?"

"Because when you love and care about someone, you don't consider being committed to them as tempting fate."

"It is tempting fate. You're going to want me to always be this guy, but I can't promise to always be this guy. Things change." He pointed to the prescription on the counter. "I'm going to change."

"I love you. That won't affect the way I feel."

"You say that now, but it will. I've been there twice already."

She glared at him. "You accused me of comparing you to Julio. Well, guess what, genius? I'm not Sabrina or Hanna. You can't expect for things between us to go the way they did with them."

"I can't hope for them to be any different, Jasmine. I don't want to do that again."

The words hurt. Dug into her heart and clawed

through the muscle with ten-inch serrated nails. He didn't love her. If he did, he wouldn't be afraid to try again. Julio had put her heart through an emotional meat shredder, but here she was. In love with Kevin and willing to try again. Her instincts this morning were right. She needed to end this.

"I've had fun, but it's gotten to the point where the fun isn't enough. I can't stick around knowing this is all you want."

"So you're gonna end this? Breaking off the good thing we've got going?"

He said the words as if she were the one being unreasonable. As if her giving up disappointed him, but there was also resignation in his eyes. He'd expected her to be disappointed and leave.

"See, that's the thing, Kevin. This has been good enough for you. It's not good enough for me anymore."

Chapter 19

Jasmine stared at the various pictures of homes and cabins she'd photographed over the summer. When she'd first taken the pictures, the homes all looked interesting and full of hidden stories just waiting to be told. Now they all looked the same.

She couldn't decide on what shots to use for the show, and worse, she was starting to believe none of the shots were good. The sunlight streaming through the windows of the office in her apartment only shone light on her foolish endeavor. That the laughter once the pictures were on display would be heard even in Milan where the fashion world would joke about how Jasmine Hook, once darling photographer of the style industry, had fallen off.

She covered her eyes with her hands and leaned her elbows on the desk. She'd been back home for a month, and even though she'd thrown herself into her work, this week she'd slammed into a brick wall of anxiety and self-doubt. This was the week she'd also slowed down enough to accept she and Kevin were through. He'd texted her at first. Tried to keep the banter they'd developed over the summer going. Even asked her to meet him in Atlanta again.

She'd ignored all the messages. He knew what she wanted and in none of his texts did he broach the subject of them being more than friends with benefits. This week, his texts and calls had stopped. One month and he'd given up and moved on. More proof she'd been way more involved in this than he'd been.

Well, it's not like you texted him back.

True. But when his texts amounted to Hey. What are you doing? Will you meet me in ATL? what was she supposed to do? They were adults. He should have called. Would have called if he really wanted to see her.

The doorbell to her apartment rang. Letting out an indignant huff, Jasmine straightened and stomped out of her office to the door. She was not in the mood to entertain anyone. However, another miniscule piece of her, one that didn't want to admit Kevin not texting might be the reason for her current creative slump, welcomed the distraction.

She peered through the peephole and sighed. Jada stood on the other side of the door. Jasmine considered not answering.

"I know you're there, so you might as well open up."

Jasmine rolled her eyes and smiled. She flipped the dead bolt and took the chain off the door. "I'm working," was her not-quite-grumbling greeting.

Jada didn't pause. She pushed past Jasmine and entered the apartment. "Take a break. You've been working like crazy since you got home."

"Because I have a show in a few weeks and I want to make sure everything is great."

"Your show is two months away. You don't have to freak out right now," Jada called over her shoulder as she waltzed her happy tail straight into Jasmine's kitchen.

Jasmine didn't follow her sister into the kitchen. That way lay cookies, potato chips and vodka. Her three crutches whenever she felt down. She slid across the floor to her couch. "Two months isn't that far away. Besides, this is important. There is no set start time for freaking out."

Rustling noises came from the kitchen, followed by the sound of the fridge opening and closing. A few seconds later, Jada emerged with a bag of chips and two bottles of water. "Which means you're really in freak-out mode because it's important to you."

Jada sauntered over and plopped onto the couch next to Jasmine. She tossed one of the bottles to her before opening the bag of chips. Jada tilted the bag toward her sister. As if she could resist potato chips. She reached in and pulled out a couple of the addictive salty treats.

"It's my first show," Jasmine said after inhaling two chips. "This is my chance to do something bigger than photograph models and celebrities."

"I don't know why traveling the world taking pictures of beautiful people and clothes was a problem for you anyway."

"It wasn't a problem. I got an idea to do something different and I couldn't stop until I tried. I want these pictures to do more than just entertain. I want them to tell a story. This is a chance for my pictures to do that."

Jada looked around Jasmine's living area. A multitude of prints were scattered around the room, an attempt to see if a different environment with different lighting would make inspiration hit. Jada frowned and then looked Jasmine over as if she were inspecting a new car.

"What the hell is really going on with you?" Jada asked her eyes narrowed. "Have you showered today?"

Jasmine slowly lifted the collar of her T-shirt to her nose and took a deep breath. So maybe she hadn't showered today. And she'd worn the same lucky top for the past two days, but she was an artist. Artists were allowed some eccentricities. She thought better when she wore this top.

Jada raised a brow and Jasmine quickly lowered the collar. "I'm nervous about the show. That's all."

"What do we need to do to get you un-nervous? When are you seeing Kevin again?"

Jasmine's stomach flexed. This conversation wasn't supposed to go there. "I thought you didn't like Kevin," she retorted.

"At least when you spend a weekend with him, you're happy again." Jada ate a few more chips.

Jasmine pretended the ache in her heart wasn't growing infinitely stronger with each passing moment and flicked her bangs out of her face with what she hoped looked like nonchalance. "I won't be spending any more weekends with Kevin. We're done."

"What happened?" Jada held the bag toward Jasmine.

"Exactly what you said would happen." Jasmine dug in and pulled out a handful. "I wanted more. He didn't."

"Did he say that?"

"Basically, after telling his ex-wife that he wasn't

marrying me and didn't have any plans to consider marrying me in the future."

She didn't go into the other issue of Kevin not trusting her to still care for him if she knew about his diagnosis. Yes, Kevin was a vibrant, athletic, magnetic man, but she'd fallen for him for other reasons. The way he hadn't freaked out the first time he'd seen her levels go low, how he supported her project, the way he made her laugh.

"Ouch," Jada said with a grimace.

"We finally had it out the last time I was in Atlanta. I told him I couldn't keep playing for fun anymore. When he didn't want to even label what we had as an official relationship, I walked away."

"Good for you. You shouldn't stick around for something you don't want."

"I don't know. Am I being crazy? We'd only been hooking up for a few months. Was I asking for too much too soon?"

Jada shook her head and held up a hand. "Don't go down that slope. There is nothing wrong with telling a guy what you want in a relationship. Otherwise, you're sitting there silently accepting a situation that isn't completely satisfying to you. You want to be with someone who loves you and isn't afraid to love you. There's nothing wrong with that."

"I know. I'm just…" She missed him. She missed him so much. This would pass. She'd get over him and she'd move on. She had to because to pine after a guy who didn't love her was crazy. "Look, can we talk about anything other than this?"

Jada cringed. Jasmine cocked her head to the side. "What's that look for?"

"I met with Kathy. You need to talk to her."

Jasmine dropped her head back. She had said *anything.* "Why?"

"Because there is more to the story. She went through a lot after her and Dad split. You should hear her out. She still cares."

"I don't want to hear her out."

"You'd rather hold on to your anger and pain? Don't. Life is short, and I know she's not our biological mom but she was our mom for nearly ten years. She raised us and she deserves to be heard."

"I don't trust her."

"I'm not asking you to trust her, I'm asking you to talk to her. I think you two will have a lot more in common than you think."

"Doubtful," Jasmine said with a snort.

"Don't doubt it. You told me that Julio's oldest daughter follows you on Instagram. She's still interested in you and she still cares, but you're staying away because Julio and his wife are back together. That sounds similar to what happened with Kathy."

Jasmine lifted a finger and gave her sister the side eye. "Don't compare me with Kathy. It's not the same."

"Isn't it? Look, she'll be back in town this weekend. Talk to her. Not because I asked you to but for your own closure." She stared at Jasmine. "Stop being afraid to trust people."

You don't trust me. Kevin had said that in his defense of them not being serious. He still had his own issues with trust and commitment, but his assessment had stung. She was afraid to trust. Afraid of being pushed aside and forgotten again. Maybe she did need closure.

Jasmine sighed. "Fine. I'll talk to her."

Chapter 20

Jasmine spotted her stepmother the second she walked into the restaurant. Even if Kathy hadn't waved and grinned when Jasmine walked through the door, she would have recognized her. Despite the years that passed, Kathy hadn't changed much. Her hair, always dyed a honey color, was shorter in a style that complemented her heart-shaped face. Her smile was still wide, open and welcoming. The smile that had greeted Jasmine after school for years. A smile that had always made her think things would be okay no matter what happened during the day.

Until that smile was no longer in her life.

Jasmine took a deep breath. She'd promised her sister she'd be here so she was here. She would only stay for a few minutes. She hadn't promised to stay for a long time.

"Hi, Kathy," Jasmine said after she walked over to the table.

Kathy's light brown eyes tightened. The brightness of her smile dimmed before she forced the sunshine back. Jasmine pushed aside the wave of guilt. Years had passed. She couldn't be expected to still call her Mom.

"Jasmine, it's so great to see you."

Kathy opened her arms. Jasmine leaned in and accepted the hug. It felt weird and comforting to be in Kathy's embrace again, surrounded by the citrus and peppermint smell of her perfume. Jasmine had to fight the urge to squeeze her tight.

She stood back quickly. "Yeah…it has been a long time." She pulled out her chair and sat.

Kathy sank back into her seat. "I know."

Irritation scratched across Jasmine's skin. She didn't want to do small talk. Didn't want to pretend only a few days had passed instead of several years. The waitress headed in their direction. She took their drink orders and walked away.

"That's what we're here to talk about, right? Why you walked away and never contacted us again?"

Kathy's hands trembled as she straightened the silverware and the water glass in front of her. "Just diving right in."

"Yes. That's the only reason I'm here."

Kathy's steady gaze met hers. "Jasmine, I didn't mean to hurt you or your sister."

Intention didn't absolve Kathy of the hurt she'd inflicted. "But you did. We were young when our mother died. You were our mother regardless of what you may have thought. When you walked away, that hurt."

"It was never my intention to walk away."

"Then why did you?" The pain-filled words spilled out and landed heavily between them.

"My heart was broken," Kathy said simply. "Your dad really hurt me, and I couldn't be around him anymore. I wasn't sure if the pain would eventually fade, but it did. By the time I woke up from the depression caused by our divorce, a year had passed. I reached out to him about you girls. He said it was too late. That I had no rights because I never legally adopted you two and he didn't want me to come around."

Jasmine loved her dad, but she also accepted that he was imperfect. They'd never gotten the story about why he and Kathy divorced, just that they didn't love each other anymore and Kathy was leaving. Her dad could hold a grudge, and if Kathy hadn't contacted him in a year, then he would have moved on. Still.

"Why would he do that?" she asked quietly. Her dad had known how much she and Jada had missed Kathy.

"I don't know. I don't think he expected me to stay away for so long. I can't put it all on him, though." Kathy's voice was filled with years of uncertainty. "It was easier for me to stay away than fight him to see you girls. I knew you'd be confused. Hurt by my decision. Especially your sister."

"Easier because you didn't love us?" Jasmine hated that her old teenage pain entered the question.

Kathy looked up quickly. She reached for Jasmine's hand on the table, but Jasmine pulled back. Kathy's mouth tightened, pain filled her eyes and she slid her hand back.

"No. That wasn't it. Your dad's words angered me. They hurt me, but they were also the truth. You weren't my kids. I wished I had insisted on the adoption, but when I married your father, I thought we were forever." She lifted and lowered a brow. "Silly me, I guess."

"It's not silly to expect your marriage to last," Jasmine countered. "I'd like to think some people still believe in forever. Still want it."

"That's true. Your dad and I were great. It wasn't until later I realized I wasn't the woman he really wanted to be with." Kathy waved her hand when Jasmine's eyes widened. "No, he didn't cheat. Your dad met me too soon after your mother died. He was still heartbroken, and unsure of what to do with two young girls. He fell in love with the idea of having a wife to help him raise you two. Not with me.

"I can't even be angry about that. I knew he was still in love with your mom, but I was in love with him. And after nine and a half years, I wanted more, and he realized he'd never been in love with me. The divorce was amicable, but the pain of knowing he still didn't love me after eleven years was too much. I'm sorry I didn't try harder to stay in your lives. I wanted what he couldn't provide. I found that and I was happy."

The waitress returned with their drinks. When she asked if they were ready to order, Kathy shook her head. "We need a few minutes."

Jasmine looked down at the menu, her mind whirling with what Kathy said. That and an echo of Jada's voice taunting *I told you so.* Jasmine could relate to Kathy's situation and her feelings. The pain of the past didn't lessen, but the anger did.

"Jada told me you that you and your husband divorced."

Kathy sighed and stirred a pack of sugar into her tea. "Midlife crisis, a red sports car and a woman twenty years younger," she said sarcastically. "Very cliché, but clichés happen for a reason."

Before she realized what she was doing, Jasmine's hand was on top of Kathy's across the table. "I'm sorry that happened."

Kathy flipped her hand over and clasped Jasmine's. "I didn't tell you that for sympathy. It's what happened. The end of that marriage made me reevaluate a lot of things in my life. I love my children, and they've gotten through this divorce with minimal collateral damage. Despite all of the years, I never stopped thinking of you and your sister. I looked you up online. Followed your careers. My kids know about you and my daughter wants to meet you."

Jasmine couldn't hide her surprise. "She does? Why?"

"Because I raised you for nine years. She says you're like sisters. She's the romantic one obviously."

"Is that why you reached out to us? Because your daughter wants to meet us?"

"No, because I needed to see you and tell you what happened. I needed to tell you I'm sorry for walking away, but I also hope you understand. If you never want to see me after this, that's fine. I just wanted to see you again."

Jasmine thought about everything Kathy had told her. She hated when her baby sister was right. She could understand Kathy's reasoning, even if she didn't like it.

Julio's kids had worked their way into her heart, but when Julio said she couldn't contact them anymore, she'd respected his wishes because she wasn't their mother. Kathy had nine years to Jasmine's eighteen months with Julio, but that didn't necessarily mean she would have had it easier to force her way into Jasmine's and Jada's lives.

The years without Kathy couldn't be erased. The

unflinching trust she'd once had wouldn't return after one lunch conversation. But Jasmine couldn't pretend she hadn't missed her. As surreal as their meeting was right now, she still hadn't taken her hand from Kathy's.

The urge to blurt out all the things happening with her was like a balloon swelling in her throat. She wanted to tell her about her concerns with the exhibit. Her creative block after realizing Kevin no longer wanted to try. Ask if she was crazy for expecting a man like Kevin to admit that he was in love with her.

She swallowed all the questions. She'd get through lunch. Being here with Kathy might make her feel as if she once again had a mother, but Jasmine was shrewd enough to accept that Kathy was maybe going through her own midlife crisis and was in the middle of reflecting on the decisions she'd made in the past. This need to be with her and Jada again could pass.

She didn't deserve all of Jasmine's pain and secrets. Maybe one day she would, but not now.

"Tell me about your kids," Jasmine said. She slipped her hand from Kathy's and leaned back in her seat. She caught the waitress's eye and waved her back over. "We're ready to order now."

Kathy relaxed and smiled. Jasmine smiled back.

Chapter 21

Kevin was father of the year.

At least, that's what his daughters and their friends said after Raymond sang happy birthday to Asia. The party was going off without a hitch. Asia was on cloud nine and his ex-wife had finally relaxed and breathed. Today was a good day.

Having Jasmine here would make it better.

The unwanted thought rushed through his head. He had a lot of unwanted thoughts about Jasmine. A week ago, he'd finally stopped texting and calling her. Pretending as if their conversation hadn't happened wasn't going to fix this. He knew what it would take, but he wasn't sure if he could do it.

Pain was a dull ache in the joints of his hands. He looked down at them. His own fault. He'd forgotten to take his medicine today in all the hubbub of Asia's party. Some days he could forget that his body was fighting itself. That he was getting old. That he'd be a burden on Jasmine one day if he gave her what she wanted. She had her own thing. She didn't need his problems.

I thought you were smarter than this. I thought you would realize that something like this wouldn't matter to me.

The look on her face when she'd said that had convinced him she was telling the truth. She wouldn't look at his condition as a failure on his part. He couldn't use that excuse anymore. This breakup was all on him. Again.

"Well, Kevin, you've now set a bar. Mya wants Wonder Woman at her birthday party."

Kevin chuckled and looked up at Hanna. She'd brought their kids over from LA for Asia's birthday.

Birthdays were always spent with each other. That was one of the ways they tried to make sure all four kids developed closeness despite their age differences and living in different parts of the country. Holidays didn't always work out. Hanna was married now. Sabrina was engaged. They both had obligations to their spouses, but birthdays they could do. They'd insisted on it. That, combined with frequent phone calls and video chats when anything important happened, worked to keep his family close.

"I'll see what I can do about that," Kevin said.

Hanna laughed and sat next to Kevin. They were in Sabrina's backyard, which had been turned into an outdoor concert hall. Sabrina hadn't done bad for herself. Her fiancé was a television producer, and from the looks of things, he loved Sabrina and the girls. He'd been just as excited and nervous as Sabrina to make Asia's birthday party a hit.

"Don't forget you've got four kids," Hanna said, flipping her thick long hair over her shoulder.

"And I'll do what I can to make birthdays special. They're the only days of the year when we're all together."

"But it won't be this way forever," Hanna said a bit wistfully. "Asia is already sixteen. I've heard her talk about design school in Paris. They're growing up so fast."

Kevin felt a tightness in his chest. He'd heard the design-school-in-Paris wish, too. *Jasmine would know the ins and out of the fashion industry.* "I know."

"What are you going to do when they are all grown up?"

He shrugged. "Celebrate."

Hanna shook her head. "Sure. We all will. But you know what I mean."

"Actually, I don't. What are you getting at?"

Hanna rubbed her hands together. Her dark, almond-shaped eyes watched him warily. "I talked to Sabrina about Jasmine."

Kevin sat up straight. "What?" His exes were discussing his defunct love life now?

"Calm down. She was upset about Asia hanging out with her. I told her the twins met Jasmine over the summer at your grandmother's house."

"Are you going to yell at me for letting the kids meet her, too?"

Hanna let out an amused sound. "No. I spoke with your grandmother. I know it wasn't *the* introduction. Your grandmother likes her. A lot."

"She does." She and his mom were here for the party, and both had asked him about Jasmine. Charlotte had looked particularly disappointed when he'd said Jasmine wasn't coming around.

"She thinks you like her a lot, too."

He looked away from Hanna's probing gaze and tried to appear indifferent. Even though his insides twisted. "We were cool."

Hanna scoffed. "Don't tell me you let her go?"

"What do you mean, let her go? She broke things off."

Hanna patted his leg as if he were a misguided kid. "Kevin, sometimes you're clueless. Why do you think I left you?"

"You said because I didn't love you."

"And I had hoped you'd fight to keep me. You didn't, and I had my answer. I'm okay with that. I'm much happier now."

Kevin put a hand over his heart. "You're cold as hell."

"It's the truth. We knew we were coming to an end. The twins kept us together a little longer, but now that I'm with Lee, I see how much better a relationship can be. I thought that because you let her meet your kids that you really cared about Jasmine. I guess I was wrong." She stood and walked away to talk to someone else.

Kevin considered her words. He did care about Jasmine. More than he'd cared about any other woman in years. That's why he'd let her break things off. Wasn't it better to end things before she realized he wasn't good at relationships?

He spotted Sabrina carrying a tray laden with cupcakes toward the house. There were plenty of people hired to help, but Sabrina had never been able to sit around and ignore something that needed to be done.

He jogged over and took the tray out of her hand. "Let me ask you a question."

Sabrina smiled as she handed over the tray and rubbed her lower back. "After making our daughter the happiest sixteen-year-old in the northern hemisphere, ask me anything."

He followed her as she continued to walk toward the house. "When we agreed to the divorce, did you want me to fight to make our marriage work?"

Sabrina stopped in her tracks. She turned to him with a wary expression. "Whoa, that's not what I expected."

"Just… I need to know."

She shrugged. "I don't know. I guess a part of me hoped you would realize you didn't want to end our marriage. Why?"

"Jasmine broke up with me."

Sabrina nodded and started for the house again. "Ah…that's what this is about."

Kevin walked with her. "Yeah, she wants more."

"Kevin, only you can decide if you want to give her more. I was mad when you brought her around Asia, but after talking to Hanna and your grandmother, I understand. You love her."

Kevin froze. "I didn't say that."

Sabrina raised a brow over her shoulder. "You don't have to say it." She continued to the house. Kevin blinked a few times, then followed. When he reached her side, Sabrina kept talking. "You don't bring the women you typically date to your grandmother's home. Much less let them meet your kids. I knew it would happen one day." She cocked her head to the side. "Funny, I thought I'd feel differently about it."

They reached the back door. He maneuvered the tray to open the door for her. "How did you think you'd feel?"

"Angry. Jealous. Upset," she said without any remorse. "I didn't feel that way when you and Hanna started dating. I knew that wasn't love."

Inside, the kitchen was quieter. Everyone, including some of the catering company, had gone outside to see and meet Raymond. Kevin set the tray on one of the granite countertops. "How did you know?"

"Come on, I like Hanna, but the two of you didn't have much in common then or now. She's beautiful and you were still in your I-just-moved-from-the-country-and-now-I'm-a-millionaire stage."

"Jesus, Sabrina, you make me sound vain." He ran a hand over his jaw but smiled at the teasing spark in her eye.

Sabrina laughed. "You're a guy. Guys like beautiful women. I couldn't exactly be pissed because you liked Hanna. She wasn't some sleazy gold digger or a beauty with no brains. So, yeah, even though I was a little *of course he's with her* when you got together, I never believed you loved her."

"Jasmine is beautiful. And she's got brains. How do you know this thing with her isn't just me succumbing to my dumb male brain?"

Sabrina crossed her arms and leaned a hip on the counter. When she looked at Kevin, her face was serious. "Because you're not just dating Jasmine. You kinda introduced her into your life. You didn't do that with Hanna until after she had the twins. By then, she was family, and though it took me a while to admit this, you're big on family. With Jasmine, you brought her into your world, your real world in Silver Springs, no strings attached. And you haven't been jet-setting out of the country with some new supermodel or partying hard with your teammates this summer. You spent it with her. Now you're actually pining over her. I never thought I'd see that."

"I'm not pining," he said, affronted by the accusation. He tugged on his shirt and twisted his neck.

Sabrina rolled her eyes. "Yes you are. I heard you mumble something about Jasmine would like that. You didn't think anyone heard, but I did. You miss her."

Damn Sabrina for being so observant. "Of course I miss her. I spent the summer with her. I got to know her. I want to make sure she's okay. That she's taking her insulin. That she's not having a hard time picking the photos for her exhibit later this year. I just want to check in and she won't even accept my calls or texts."

Sabrina laughed. "Kevin, why are you so afraid to love this woman?"

"Because I loved you and I hurt you. Hanna loved me and I hurt her. I don't want to do that to Jasmine."

Sabrina's smile turned sad. "You're such a man. Kevin, you're hurting her now. Look, our divorce was… screwed up. And your breakup with Hanna came nine months too late, but you can't keep guarding yourself from falling in love again. Just don't mess up this time."

"I don't know if I won't. My dad—"

"Your dad is a jerk who walked away from his family and only tried to look back when you entered the league," Sabrina said forcefully. "You aren't him. We were too young when we got married. We both know that. I was hurt, but I get it. I was your first, for God's sake. You wanted to experience life, and honestly, I got to experience life too after our divorce." She patted his arm. "The only way you're going to be like your dad is if you run away when things get hard. And the guy I know, the one with multiple championships, who's played hard since he was eighteen and for the past few years has always been there to make his children happy, shouldn't be afraid of that."

She squeezed his arm and walked out of the kitchen. Kevin felt as if he'd been knocked off his feet.

"She's right, you know," his grandmother's voice came from the door of the kitchen.

Kevin continued to stare at the spot Sabrina had been. "I was so afraid I was like him."

"It's time for you to heal, baby," Charlotte said.

He finally looked at his grandmother, saw the love and hope in her eyes that made his chest ache. "From what?"

"From your breakups with Sabrina and Hanna. They hurt you, too, but don't let that break you. Be happy."

Maybe he'd already screwed things up with Jasmine. There was no guarantee she'd take him back, but did he really want to give up and not try? He didn't take a simple defeat on the court. Why should he admit defeat now? If he had screwed things up, he could find a way to fix things, too.

He smiled at his grandmother. "I will."

Chapter 22

Jasmine invited Jada over to celebrate her victory. She'd finally gotten out of her own head and selected the photos she wanted to use for the show. The celebration consisted of the two of them with wine and popcorn in Jasmine's living room, but it felt like Jasmine's birthday. She was filled with thankfulness, optimism and the urge to toast good fortune.

"What helped you finally pick the shots?" Jada asked. She had her feet propped up on Jasmine's coffee table. The window was open to let out the smell of the first bag of microwave popcorn Jasmine had burned. The city sounds drifted in. "Not that I mind coming over for an early-afternoon wine celebration."

"I had to get out of my own head. Plus, when Angelo from the Angelero Gallery called last week to confirm some of the details, it hit me I couldn't doubt myself. He was excited and that reminded me that I wouldn't have gotten the offer to exhibit or the book deal if others didn't believe in my project, too. I can't let everyone down."

"Well, here's to overcoming obstacles." Jada raised her glass. "And to overcoming misconceptions."

Jasmine rolled her eyes. "Will you stop being smug for half a day?"

"No. I knew you'd be glad you met with Kathy."

"You were right. It was good for me to hear her side of the story. I still don't like her decisions, but I needed to hear her out."

Jada's smug look gave way to hesitation. "Are you going to say anything to Dad?"

Jasmine had spoken to her dad after meeting with Kathy. Though the questions had bubbled in her chest, she hadn't voiced them. "Not yet. When he called, he was so happy about the promotion at his job. I'm still upset that he didn't let Kathy see us when she first asked. A part of me is angry, but I didn't want to argue with him and ruin his day."

"And the other part?" Jada asked.

Jasmine took a sip of wine. "Understands he was also trying to protect us, I guess. He didn't know what keeping Kathy in our lives would result in. I can't let my pain over Kathy not being around cloud my judgment when I ask for his side of the story. I'll talk with him about it soon."

Jada tilted her head to the side. Her eyes lit with admiration. "Look at you, being grown and reasonable."

"Is that so hard to believe?"

"Not really. Sometimes I think you're reasonable when you should freak out a little. Kathy told me you invited her to your showing."

"I did. I'll talk with Dad before then. That way he isn't blindsided when she shows up."

"They haven't seen each other in a long time."

"Don't get any crazy fanciful ideas." Their dad had also been excited about a new woman he'd met. Though he hadn't dated seriously since divorcing Kathy, and Jasmine wasn't sure if he ever wanted to marry again, she did want her dad to have a companion and find happiness.

Jada tried to look innocent. "Who said I had ideas?"

Jasmine's cell phone rang. She narrowed her eyes at Jada as she picked up her phone. "Dad is happy now. Don't stir up old stuff that needs to be left alone." She looked at the number on the screen. It was the gallery. She held up a finger to Jada, silently asking her sister to hold her next comment, and answered, "Hello?"

"Jasmine, hi. It's Angelo. I had to call you immediately. I have another artist here interested in showing his work in my gallery. The only problem is he wants to show at the same time as you."

Jasmine sat up abruptly on the couch. The bag of popcorn in her lap spilling onto the floor. "That's too bad for him, because I've already been scheduled."

"I know, but he's insistent that you give up a week, and I'm a little interested in what he's offering."

"Are you serious? You can't be willing to kick me out." Jasmine had known Angelo for years and never would have expected him to drop one exhibit in favor of another. Not this late in the game anyway.

"I'd like you to come over so we can discuss this in person."

"Who is he?" Only a few people in the industry had that much weight. She was popular, but if there was a player big enough to oust her, she was going to have to prepare for a fight.

"Just come down and let's talk. I'll tell you everything when you get here."

"I'm coming now." She ended the call and stood, brushing crumbs off her torn jeans onto the floor.

"What's wrong?" Jada asked.

"Some jerk is trying to take over my time at the gallery. I've got to go down there and straighten this out." She was already looking for her purse and keys.

"Can they do that?"

Jasmine glared at her sister. "Not if I have anything to say about it."

She was out of her apartment in an instant. She fumed as she flagged down a taxi. How could Angelo do this to her? They'd been friends for years. He had been just as excited about showing Jasmine's new work as Jasmine had. Now he was ready to dump Jasmine for someone else?

Oh no. She wasn't giving up a second of her time for anyone. Regardless of who they were. She'd had enough to deal with this summer without the added disappointment of losing her opportunity to at least make her professional life something worth fighting for.

The taxi finally arrived, and Jasmine's hot anger hadn't chilled. After the trip, she paid, shot out of the car like a bullet and marched to the gallery. She snatched open the door, not paying attention to the Closed sign or the fact that Angelero wasn't usually closed this early on a Saturday.

She marched through the door. "Angelo, we need to talk now."

She looked around for Angelo, ready to fight despite

their years of friendship, then froze. She sucked in a breath. Her purse thudded to the floor.

The open exhibit space was filled with pictures of her and Kevin. The first selfie they'd taken when he'd told her she was beautiful in pictures. Photos he'd snapped of her when he thought she wasn't paying attention to him. Silly moments they'd had together as he'd shown her around Silver Springs. Her talking to his grandmother and laughing with Rachel and Tank. Their victory picture with the certificates Angela had given out at couples game night.

Tears burned in her eyes and throat. She placed a hand over her pounding heart. "What's this?"

"The only way I could think of to get you to talk to me," Kevin's voice came from behind.

Jasmine closed her eyes. She sucked in a shaky breath as her body buzzed with awareness. She slowly faced him. Her heart clenched the second she saw him. A crisp white button-up molded to his body and navy slacks accentuated his strong legs. "You did this?"

He took a few steps toward her. "Angelo helped. Don't worry. No one is stopping your exhibit."

"Why? Why did you do this?" She kept her voice strong. Hid the tumult of emotions bouncing inside of her. Excitement, hope, love.

He stopped a few steps away. Dark eyes met hers with such focus she wanted to run to him. Wrap her arms around him. Tell him how much she'd hurt in the time they'd been apart.

"Because I needed to show you how I felt. Telling you wasn't enough. I always thought I was bad at relationships. I thought it was the only thing my dad left me. My marriage didn't work, I couldn't love Hanna, I figured I was broken. Then the diagnosis came, and I thought my body, the thing I made my living with, was abandoning me, too. I didn't think I was worth loving."

"That's not true." Her anger at him for thinking that crept into her voice.

He nodded. "I know that. I accept that. I've been… guarding myself. I didn't realize that until recently. The divorce, hurting Hanna, those things hurt me, too. I was afraid of failing, hurting again."

Hope was like sunshine in her heart. "And now?"

He stepped closer. "If I don't try, then I've already failed. I love you, Jasmine. I didn't want to admit it. Didn't want to believe it because I haven't felt this way before. I don't know what the future holds, or how things will progress with me, but I know I want you by my side as I take this next step in my life. If you'll have me."

"Kevin, that day you accused me of not trusting you…"

"I was frustrated."

She shook her head. "No, you were right. People I love have left me. My mother died, Kathy moved on." She took a deep breath. "And, yes, Julio tore my heart in half. I took that out on you. I don't want you to ever think that I'm not supportive of you and your family. I was looking for trouble where there wasn't any. I do trust you. I love you, and I'm sorry."

Strong arms wrapped around her and pulled her close into his embrace. Jasmine lifted up on her toes and kissed him, her heart near to bursting with excitement and joy.

He pulled back and looked into her eyes. "I love you. I will do everything I can to make you happy."

She glanced around at the pictures. Looked back into his dark eyes and knew that she wouldn't want to be with anyone else. "You're already off to a good start."

Chapter 23

A strong arm slid around Jasmine's midsection before her back was pressed against Kevin's solid chest. She smiled and leaned into him. He lowered his head and kissed her cheek.

"I told you everything was going to be okay," he whispered in her ear.

Jasmine let out a deep satisfying breath. The turnout for her showing was bigger than she'd expected. Not only had the expected art critics and regulars of the gallery come out to see the new exhibit, but her publisher had put out the word to several of her colleagues, some of the celebrities she'd photographed in her career and, the biggest surprise, a few history professors from colleges in the city. The only laughter in the building came from people having a good time. She'd gotten nothing but positive feedback and encouragement.

"I still can't believe they get what I was trying to portray," she said.

Kevin rested his chin on the top of her head. "I got what you were trying to portray the second you explained your project to me. You did what you set out to do. You've shone a light on a segment of history. Enjoy the moment."

"I guess we've both surprised ourselves."

Kevin's first segment on *Sports Reporter* had aired the week before. He'd done exactly what the producers had hoped he would: brought energy and a new perspective to the long-standing show. The ratings had jumped, and fans had engaged with Kevin and the other hosts on social media throughout the show.

"There is a life for me after basketball," Kevin said. "And apparently there is a life for you outside of fashion photography."

She turned in his arms and grinned up at him. He'd taken her breath away in the bold and stylish maroon fitted suit he'd worn to the showing.

They'd been late because she'd immediately begun undressing him right after he'd gotten the suit on. Not that he'd seemed to mind. The zipper of her wine-colored maxi dress had been broken in Kevin's haste to get her undressed. Thank goodness for safety pins, but she'd almost regretted wearing the backless dress. The open back and side cutouts left way too much skin for Kevin to caress and tease when they stood next to each other. Completely distracting her from important conversations.

"I don't think I'll completely give up fashion photography," she said. "I still love the work. I never found it unfulfilling, but now I know that if I want to try a new project, I can step out into the unknown."

"I'll always be there to support you."

She cocked a brow. "Are you sure? I can be pretty taxing when I'm trying new stuff."

She knew she'd driven everyone crazy in the final weeks leading up to the showing. So much so that Jada had refused to come over unless Kevin was there to play referee.

He'd moved to New York and traveled to Atlanta for the tapings of the show. She couldn't believe he'd taken the step. They were moving in together next week.

She didn't expect a marriage proposal anytime soon. Kevin had already been married and she knew he was leery of taking such a big step again. But outside of that, he'd done everything to make their relationship work.

"I might be able to deal with you," he said with a teasing lift of his lips. "In fact, I was thinking—"

"Jasmine, I need you for just a second. I've got three buyers interested in one of your prints and I want to talk to you about the terms of the sale."

Jasmine grinned at Angelo. "Three buyers? Of course, I'll be right there." She looked at Kevin. "I'll be back."

There was a flash of disappointment before he nodded and smiled. "Sure."

Jasmine hesitated for a second. He had been about to say something when Angelo interrupted. "Did you have to tell me something?"

"It'll wait until after you go get that money."

Jasmine laughed. "True." She lifted her chin and kissed him quickly, then followed Angelo. On the way, she smiled at her dad and Kathy. They'd both been surprisingly civil during the event. Jasmine still hadn't asked her dad about his reasons for keeping Kathy away.

That was the past and she was going to tentatively embrace the future with Kathy back in her life.

She waved at Kevin's mom and grandmother talking with Jada. The two most important women in Kevin's life had embraced her with open arms. She hadn't set out to win their hearts, but she couldn't deny that it felt good knowing she had their approval.

She was also finding her fit in Kevin's blended family. His kids liked her, and she was forming a tentative friendship with Hanna and Sabrina.

You're going to be around for good, Sabrina had said when Jasmine and Kevin were in Atlanta a month ago. *I'm glad he's finally allowed himself to be happy.*

Jasmine worked on the terms of sale with Angelo and was then swept into various conversations for the rest of the night. Before she knew it, the night was over and she'd sold every original photograph. Her editor was elated and wanted to get with Jasmine first thing in the morning to discuss publicity for the book. Jasmine was floating on a wave of happiness and gratitude that her project was turning out so well.

She and Kevin weren't alone again until they were in the car on the way back to her apartment. He'd moved in with her while they searched for a larger space to live in together.

Jasmine strolled into the apartment and kicked off her heels. "That has to be the best feeling on the planet."

"What?" Kevin asked, closing the apartment door behind her.

"Taking off heels after several hours of standing."

Kevin chuckled. He swept her off her feet and into his arms. Jasmine laughed and wrapped her arms around his neck. "I'm sure that feels great, but best feeling on the planet?"

"Well…maybe not *the* best."

"That's what I thought."

She expected him to take her into the bedroom. Instead he walked over and set her on the bar separating the living and dining spaces. "What are you doing?"

"I want to talk to you about something." There was still a spark in his eye, but his tone was serious.

"Is something wrong?"

He shook his head. "No, I've been thinking about getting a new tattoo and I want to talk to you about it."

Jasmine raised her brows. "Seriously? Another one? I mean, I love your art, but where would you even put it?"

He held up his left hand and wiggled the ring finger. "Here. I'll buy a real ring, too, but if you marry me, I know it's forever. It'll be the last tattoo I get."

If she hadn't been sitting, she would have fallen. Her stomach flipped, and her heart raced as a euphoria that topped everything else that had happened that night filled her. "Marry you? You want to get married?"

He took her hands in his. "I love you. Is it so hard to imagine I'd want to spend the rest of my life with you?"

"I didn't think you'd ever want to get married again."

"That's when I thought I wasn't good at relationships. What I know now is that what I feel for you, and what I hope to always have with you, is bigger than any fear I may have. I don't care what happens tomorrow with my health, your health, our careers or anything else as long as I know you'll be there beside me." He took a deep breath and brought their joined hands to his chest. "Jasmine, will you marry me?"

The pounding of his heart beneath her hands matched

the excited pace of her own. She knew the answer immediately. "Yes."

Kevin's grin made her feel as if she could fly. He took her face in his hands and kissed her.

Who would have thought a nude photography shoot would turn out to be the best thing to ever happen to her?

* * * * *

COMING NEXT MONTH
Available July 17, 2018

#581 ONE PERFECT MOMENT
The Taylors of Temptation • by A.C. Arthur

TV producer Ava Cannon is stunned to discover that the lover who briefly shared her bed is one of America's most famous sextuplets. But Dr. Gage Taylor now shuns the spotlight. As they rekindle their affair, will Ava have to choose between a game-changing career move and her love?

#582 CAMPAIGN FOR HIS HEART
The Cardinal House • by Joy Avery

Former foster child Lauder Tolson is running for North Carolina state senate, but he needs a girlfriend for the campaign. The ideal candidate is childhood nemesis Willow Dawson. To fulfill her own dream, she agrees. Soon, they're a devoted couple in public, but neither expects how hot it gets in private.

#583 PATH TO PASSION
The Astacios • by Nana Prah

Heir to his family's global empire, branding genius Miguel Astacio turns everything into marketing gold. Only his best friend's sister seems immune to his magic touch. Until Tanya Carrington comes to him to save her floundering nightclub. Miguel is ready to rectify past mistakes. But will he win her heart?

#584 UNCONDITIONALLY MINE
Miami Dreams • by Nadine Gonzalez

Event planner Sofia Silva is keeping a secret. No one can know that her engagement to her cheating fiancé is over. Until she meets gorgeous, wealthy newcomer Jonathan Gunther. When he invites Sofia to lie low at his house, their attraction explodes…but will her dilemma ruin their chance at forever?

Get 2 Free Books,
Plus 2 Free Gifts—
just for trying the
Reader Service!

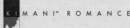

At three minutes after six, Gage was standing at the door
of the deck once more, smiling up at Ava as she stepped
slowly onto the yacht.

"You look beautiful," he said, taking her hand to help
her on board. "I'm so glad you're here."

And he was, Gage thought as he looked down into her
deep brown eyes. He was glad to see her in the short blue
dress that might have seemed plain on anyone else but
her. She wore a blue-and-beige scarf draped around her
neck and black boots to her calf. Her hair was free and
flowing so that she had a fresh and innocently enticing
look. Yes, he was glad she was here.

"I almost didn't come," she said and then shook her head as if trying to dismiss the words. "I meant to say thank you. I'm looking forward to a great evening."

He heard the words and saw the small smile she offered, but Gage wasn't buying it. Her eyes and the slight slump in her shoulders said differently.

"Is something wrong, Ava? Did something happen to you today?"

"No," she said and waved her hand over her face like she needed to wipe away whatever was bothering her. "I'm fine. It's nothing. Let's just have dinner."

"Sure. Everything's ready," Gage told her.

He led her to the table and pulled out the matching bronzed iron chair, all the while thinking that she was a horrible liar. Something was definitely wrong with her, and he was determined to find out what.

So he could fix it. Gage knew in that instant that he would do anything to take that look off her face. Anything at all.

Don't miss One Perfect Moment
by A.C. Arthur, available August 2018
wherever Harlequin® Kimani Romance™
books and ebooks are sold.

KPEXP0718

Want to give in to temptation with
steamy tales of irresistible desire?

Check out **Harlequin® Presents®,
Harlequin® Desire** and
Harlequin® Kimani™ Romance books!

New books available every month!

CONNECT WITH US AT:

Harlequin.com/Community

Facebook.com/HarlequinBooks

Twitter.com/HarlequinBooks

Instagram.com/HarlequinBooks

Pinterest.com/HarlequinBooks

ReaderService.com

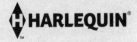

**ROMANCE WHEN
YOU NEED IT**

PGENRE2017

Reward the book lover in you!

Earn points on your purchase of new Harlequin books from participating retailers.

Turn your points into **FREE BOOKS** of your choice!

Join for FREE today at
www.HarlequinMyRewards.com.

Harlequin My Rewards is a free program (no fees) without any commitments or obligations.

MYR18